THE TRAIL TO LOVE

Elissa went back to her bed and almost at once, she found herself dreaming.

In her dream she was sitting in a green woodland glade, where long bars of sunlight shone down through the leaves, making pools of golden light on the grass.

Someone was walking towards Elissa.

A slim woman in a long white dress with a fine lace veil over her face.

She looked strangely familiar and as she drew near, Elissa saw that she was carrying a large book.

"Mama – is it you?" Elissa asked, trying to see the woman's face.

The woman approached her and laid the book in Elissa's lap.

"It *is* you, isn't it?" cried Elissa, for now she saw that the woman's beautiful slender hands were just like her mother's.

Now the woman laid one of her hands on Elissa's head just as Mama used to do.

Then she spoke in a soft voice,

"My darling – a time of great happiness is coming to you. However long the road may be, you must always remember I have told you this."

Elissa found tears welling up into her eyes as she recognised her Mama's voice.

THE BARBARA CARTLAND
PINK COLLECTION

Titles in this series

THE TRAIL TO LOVE

BARBARA CARTLAND

Barbaracartland.com Ltd

THE BARBARA CARTLAND PINK COLLECTION

Barbara Cartland was the most prolific bestselling author in the history of the world. She was frequently in the Guinness Book of Records for writing more books in a year than any other living author. In fact her most amazing literary feat was when her publishers asked for more Barbara Cartland romances, she doubled her output from 10 books a year to over 20 books a year, when she was 77.

She went on writing continuously at this rate for 20 years and wrote her last book at the age of 97, thus completing 400 books between the ages of 77 and 97.

Her publishers finally could not keep up with this phenomenal output, so at her death she left 160 unpublished manuscripts, something again that no other author has ever achieved.

Now the exciting news is that these 160 original unpublished Barbara Cartland books are already being published and by Barbaracartland.com exclusively on the internet, as the international web is the best possible way of reaching so many Barbara Cartland readers around the world.

The 160 books are published monthly and will be numbered in sequence.

The series is called the Pink Collection as a tribute to Barbara Cartland whose favourite colour was pink and it became very much her trademark over the years.

The Barbara Cartland Pink Collection is published only on the internet. Log on to www.barbaracartland.com to find out how you can purchase the books monthly as they are published, and take out a subscription that will ensure that all subsequent editions are delivered to you by mail order to your home.

NEW

Barbaracartland.com is proud to announce the publication of ten new Audio Books for the first time as CDs. They are favourite Barbara Cartland stories read by well-known actors and actresses and each story extends to 4 or 5 CDs. The Audio Books are as follows:

The Patient Bridegroom	The Passion and the Flower
A Challenge of Hearts	Little White Doves of Love
A Train to Love	The Prince and the Pekinese
The Unbroken Dream	A King in Love
The Cruel Count	A Sign of Love

More Audio Books will be published in the future and the above titles can be purchased by logging on to the website www.barbaracartland.com or please write to the address below.

If you do not have access to a computer, you can write for information about the Barbara Cartland Pink Collection and the Barbara Cartland Audio Books to the following address:

Barbara Cartland.com Ltd., Camfield Place,
Hatfield, Hertfordshire AL9 6JE, United Kingdom.

Telephone: +44 (0)1707 642629
Fax: +44 (0)1707 663041

THE LATE DAME BARBARA CARTLAND

Barbara Cartland who sadly died in May 2000 at the age of nearly 99 was the world's most famous romantic novelist who wrote 723 books in her lifetime with worldwide sales of over 1 billion copies and her books were translated into 36 different languages.

As well as romantic novels, she wrote historical biographies, 6 autobiographies, theatrical plays, books of advice on life, love, vitamins and cookery. She also found time to be a political speaker and television and radio personality.

She wrote her first book at the age of 21 and this was called *Jigsaw*. It became an immediate bestseller and sold 100,000 copies in hardback and was translated into 6 different languages. She wrote continuously throughout her life, writing bestsellers for an astonishing 76 years. Her books have always been immensely popular in the United States, where in 1976 her current books were at numbers 1 & 2 in the B. Dalton bestsellers list, a feat never achieved before or since by any author.

Barbara Cartland became a legend in her own lifetime and will be best remembered for her wonderful romantic novels, so loved by her millions of readers throughout the world.

Her books will always be treasured for their moral message, her pure and innocent heroines, her good looking and dashing heroes and above all her belief that the power of love is more important than anything else in everyone's life.

"Everything dies, decays and is forgotten, except for love which lasts for ever even into Eternity."

Barbara Cartland

CHAPTER ONE
1903

"Would you care to take a look at your post, sir?"

Travis, the elderly butler, asked, as he brought in a silver pot of steaming coffee to the breakfast table at No. 13 Lanchberry Close, Mayfair.

"There is rather a lot of it," he added.

Young Richard Stanfield sighed as he thought of the mountain of unopened envelopes on the hall table of the elegant town house in Mayfair where he had grown up.

Of course there would be very many letters as he had been away in South America for nearly three months following the death of his dear father, Sir Julius Stanfield, and with no one at the house to open them, the envelopes would just pile up.

Travis was still hovering by the table, his white whiskers drooping rather sadly.

He was probably missing Sir Julius, whom he had served faithfully for thirty years.

Richard missed him too.

Yesterday when he arrived back at his home dusty and exhausted from his long journey, he had forgotten for a moment that his father was no longer there to shout out,

"Hello old young 'un!" as he would hurry out of his study to greet his son.

"Please bring in the post, Travis, and I will open it while I drink my coffee," said Richard, and the old butler gave a nod and hobbled off to the hall to fetch the letters.

Richard finished eating the scrambled eggs, bacon, and sausage that lay on his plate – it was the first proper English food he had eaten for ages and it tasted very good.

The coffee, however, was a disappointment.

Richard had grown used to the intense dark flavour of the authentic South American blends on his travels, and the bland offering that Travis had just brought up from the kitchen was no match for it.

"Here you are, sir."

Travis laid a large tray piled high with envelopes beside Richard's coffee cup.

"Will you be requiring anything else, sir?"

Richard saw that Travis had thoughtfully provided a silver paper knife for opening the letters.

"No thank you, Travis. You may go."

He drained the last of his cup, wishing that it could have been extra strong Colombian to give him strength for the task ahead and picked up the paper knife.

The first letter he opened was from the bank.

"*Dear sir,*" it read. "*It is with regret that we must inform you that your overdraft has been exceeded – please contact us at your earliest opportunity –* "

Richard winced.

He opened the next letter and saw that it was from Boustred and Sons, gentlemen's outfitters.

"*Dear sir, our account dated the 30th September remains unpaid –* "

If only he had paid for everything when he went in to pick up the lightweight tropical suits he had ordered for his trip abroad.

2

But he did not know then how things were going to turn out.

Richard rummaged through the pile of letters and his heart sank as he could tell, even without opening them, that they were all bills and final demands for payment.

'What shall I do?' he muttered to himself, pushing the letters away. 'What on earth can I do to get myself out of this mess?'

There was a loud rat-a-tat at the front door.

Richard heard a mumble of voices in the hall and then Travis came back into the dining room.

"Mr. Bagley to see you, sir."

"Send him in," replied Richard, his heart sinking.

Mr. Bagley runs the Livery Stables just around the corner from Lanchberry Close, where Sir Julius had kept his horses for riding and carriage work.

Mr. Bagley strode into the room, sweat shining on his round red face and stood in front of Richard, clutching his bowler hat in his hands.

"Good morning to you, sir," he began sullenly.

Richard sniffed appreciatively at the odour of straw and warm horses that always seemed to follow Mr. Bagley wherever he went and remembered some happy days in his childhood when the red-faced gentleman had taught him to ride in Hyde Park, puffing along on foot after his spirited white pony, Snowball.

But Mr. Bagley was not looking at all cheerful and encouraging as he did in those days.

He was frowning and avoiding Richard's eyes.

"Your father – ahem – your late father – "

Mr. Bagley wiped his brow and seemed unable to continue.

"Oh, dear," Richard muttered. "I suppose you have come about an unpaid bill."

Mr. Bagley looked slightly relieved.

"Indeed. The situation is a difficult one. Sir Julius was poorly for sometime and I did not like to remind him that his regular payments had been missed and after the dear man passed away, you, Mr. Richard, disappeared for a very long time."

"How much is it?"

"Two hundred pounds, Mr. Richard."

"Phew!"

Richard felt quite panicky. There was absolutely no way he could find that amount of money.

"The thing is, Mr. Bagley, I am not sure that I can lay my hands on two hundred pounds right now."

Mr. Bagley shook his head.

"There's six fat horses in my stables, Mr. Richard, eating their heads off at my expense."

Richard suddenly felt a terrible emptiness.

There was really only one thing to do and he could not bear the thought of it.

"I must have my two hundred pounds. I'm not a rich man, sir, I've a wife and four daughters to keep," Mr. Bagley was now saying.

"Mr. Bagley, of course, I understand. I don't want you to suffer any hardship. But I simply don't have the money. The only thing is – I don't suppose – would you take the horses instead?"

His heart ached at the thought of Trumpeter, his father's favourite hunter and Bluebird, his own incredibly swift thoroughbred.

To say nothing about Whiskey, Brandy, Rum and Cognac, the fine brown horses that had faithfully pulled the Stanfield carriage for so many years.

Mr. Bagley turned a deeper shade of red and looked down at his boots.

"It's a kind offer, Mr. Richard, but I'd doubt they'd make two hundred pounds at market. They're old and past their best except for your Bluebird."

Now Richard felt his own face grow hot.

"I'm really sorry, Mr. Bagley. It's been a bit of a nightmare. I ran into some difficulties in South America and I'm afraid I've no ready cash at all at the moment."

Mr. Bagley straightened up and starting twisting his hat round and round in his hands.

"I'm sorry, I am sure, to hear that. Your father was a good man and my best customer till he fell ill. I'm happy to help you, Mr. Richard, by selling the horses on. I'll do my best to find good places for them. And we'll say no more about the debt."

Richard thanked him, feeling somewhat comforted.

Then suddenly he remembered the little white pony who had been his first mount and who was now living out the days of his retirement at the livery stables.

"Mr. Bagley. There is one other thing – Snowball."

The man's red face split into a wide smile.

"Aha, Mr. Richard. Don't worry about that pony. My girls adore him. He'll have a home with us and plenty of the finest hay for as long as the little beggar's got teeth to chew it!"

Richard smiled too.

The thought of Snowball being spoiled and adored by four little girls somehow made him feel better about not being able to pay Mr. Bagley properly for his services.

They shook hands and Travis led the Livery Stable manager away to the front door, leaving Richard in a sober and thoughtful mood.

He had behaved very stupidly indeed while he had been in South America and now, without a single penny of his substantial inheritance left in the bank, he was going to have to pay a hefty price for what he had done.

*

Elissa Valentine stood in the back garden, a pile of rugs over her arm and let the icy January breeze ruffle her long golden hair, blowing away her weariness and her sad thoughts.

It was a bitterly cold day, but the sun was shining down over the roofs of the pretty white houses in St. John's Wood, and she could see that the green shoots of the spring flowers were already pushing up through the soil.

She tossed the rugs over the washing line and began to beat the dust from them noticing that some were looking very worn with bare patches showing though the reds and golds of the Persian designs.

Her father, the well-known artist Leo Valentine, had loved bright colours.

All his paintings glowed with endless colour and he had insisted that everything in the house – curtains, rugs, walls – should reflect the glorious colours of flowers and birds and sunshine.

But now her beloved Papa was dead and Elissa was clearing up the house so that it could be rented out to new tenants.

Elissa missed her Papa more than she could say.

He had died so peacefully in his bed and quickly without any suffering and she knew she should feel glad about that, but he was gone and no one could ever fill his place.

She paused for a moment in her beating of the rugs and watched the dust drifting away on the breeze.

Her father had been a lion of man, over six feet tall and well built. He had a thick mane of golden hair, just the same colour as hers, and a long beard.

Many people became alarmed at Leo Valentine's unconventional appearance, as he liked to wear smoking jackets of bright purple and green velvet and when he was painting, a blue smock covered in daubs of paint.

But Elissa knew he was the kindest and gentlest of men, who had always loved her dearly and wanted nothing more than her happiness.

Over the last two years they had grown especially close, for her Papa's heart had grown unreliable and he had been unable to leave the house.

It was an effort for him even to climb the stairs to his bedroom without Elissa's arm to lean on.

There was little money in the Valentine household and just one servant worked there – a little maid called Kitty, who laid the fires and peeled the vegetables and did the heavy cleaning that was too much for Elissa.

And Elissa did everything else.

She cooked and dusted and waited on her Papa and when he became ill, she looked after him.

If her Mama had still been alive, it would have been very different. Her Papa would then have had two devoted women to care for him.

Lady Helena Hartwell, the most famous beauty of her day, had scandalised Society by marrying for love, and a poor artist to boot, but she had never regretted what she had done.

"I have been so happy with your Papa, my darling," Elissa could remember her saying some years before, as they sat cuddled up together on one of the Persian rugs in front of a blazing fire.

"I love him so very much and if I had not run away with him – why, I would never have had you, my lovely daughter!"

Elissa had asked her why her own mother and the rest of the family no longer spoke to her.

"Because they do not understand, sweetheart. They wanted me to marry a man with a title and fortune, because that was what all girls like me were expected to do. They could not see that without the love of your Papa I could never be happy. We may not have very much money, but we are together *and we have you*!"

That was one of the times after a painting had been sold, when there was a bit more prosperity in the Valentine household. There was money to pay for logs and coal and to buy a joint of meat for dinner on Sundays.

Elissa's mother was very beautiful with thick dark hair and lovely brown eyes that glowed like dark sherry.

She was slim and elegant, always full of life and fun, laughing and joking with everyone as she struggled to make ends meet.

But Lady Helena Hartwell's aristocratic sheltered upbringing had not prepared her for the hardships of being a struggling artist's wife, and for the long cold winters and the weeks when all the available money went to pay the rent and there was none left to put food on the table.

When Elissa was just twelve years old, her Mama caught a bad cold.

Then too it was bitter January weather and the rich folk who like to buy pictures to hang on their walls were staying inside their snug homes to keep warm, so there was little money coming in.

Lady Helena just could not summon the strength to recover and when finally the doctor came, he told Leo that she was gravely ill with pneumonia.

Leo was beside himself with grief and worry, but Lady Helena bore no resentment against her husband for the fact that he had no money to light a fire in her room or to call the doctor out more often.

"One day," she whispered to Elissa, smiling as she lay back on her snowy pillows, "your Papa will be very famous. His genius will be discovered and everyone will want one of his marvellous paintings. It is just a question of time – "

Not long after she said this, she took her last breath, held closely in her husband's arms.

*

The artist clung very tightly to his little girl, Elissa, in the years that followed.

He worked harder than ever to sell his work, for he felt that if he had been more successful and earned more money perhaps he would not have lost his beloved wife.

And Elissa then most gladly stepped into the role of housekeeper and companion to her father, for to her he was the most wonderful man in the world, who brought beauty and joy and excitement to whatever he did.

But after a while the artist grew ill and weak with a heart condition and his bright mane of hair began to turn grey.

He still painted, but Elissa recognised that it was a tremendous effort for him to keep standing up for long hours in front of his easel.

One morning after he had been unwell for several months, Elissa woke very early.

The winter sky was still dark over St. John's Wood as the sun had not yet risen.

She jumped quickly out of bed, suddenly anxious for her Papa and ran to his room to check that all was well with him.

"Papa?" she called from the door, but he was fast asleep, a mound of quilts and blankets piled over him and he was breathing deeply and peacefully.

Elissa went back to her bed and almost at once, she found herself dreaming.

In her dream she was sitting in a green woodland glade, where long bars of sunlight shone down through the leaves, making pools of golden light on the grass.

Someone was walking towards Elissa.

A slim woman in a long white dress with a fine lace veil over her face.

She looked strangely familiar and as she drew near, Elissa saw that she was carrying a large book.

"Mama – is it you?" Elissa asked, trying to see the woman's face.

The woman approached her and laid the book in Elissa's lap.

"It *is* you, isn't it?" cried Elissa, for now she saw that the woman's beautiful slender hands were just like her mother's.

Now the woman laid one of her hands on Elissa's head just as Mama used to do.

Then she spoke in a soft voice,

"My darling – a time of great happiness is coming to you. However long the road may be, you must always remember I have told you this."

Elissa found tears welling up into her eyes as she recognised her Mama's voice.

"But – Papa is not well – I am frightened for him, Mama – every day I pray for him and I hope that he will be better – but the doctors say it is his heart and there is no cure."

"Do not be afraid, my darling," her Mama replied, and she bent and opened the book, which she had placed in Elissa's lap. "Your Papa is deeply loved. All will be well with him and he will soon be home."

Elissa's dream-self struggled to comprehend what was happening.

She half-remembered that just a moment ago, she had seen her father sleeping in his bedroom.

Of course he was at home!

Now the white-clad figure was leaving her, walking away from her across the sunlit grass.

"*Mama*! Wait!"

Elissa struggled to get up, but in the peculiar way that sometimes happens in dreams, her legs would not obey her and she fell back onto the soft grass.

She looked down at the book and saw that it was some kind of calendar. It lay open at the page for the 24th of December, Christmas Eve.

And beneath the date was written her Papa's name, Leo Valentine.

Now just four months later standing out in the cold garden with no coat on, Elissa shivered.

How strange it was to think that her Papa had really died on Christmas Eve.

And why had she had that dream, which had felt both sad and joyful at the same time?

She must stop dithering.

It was cold and time to finish beating dust out of the old rugs and take them back inside.

"Miss Elissa, will you no 'ave a cup of tea?" Kitty asked her as they spread the rugs out over the wooden floor in the hall. "It's right perishin' out 'ere."

"Thank you, dear Kitty. I would love one."

"You're workin' far too 'ard, miss," said Kitty, a frown on her thin face. "Take the weight off your feet for five minutes."

Elissa laughed.

It was so touching the way that the young maid was being so motherly towards her.

She ran in and went into the drawing room and sat on the battered old sofa, where she could look up at the portrait of her Mama that Papa had painted many years ago before they were married.

Helena's aristocratic family, the owners of a vast estate in East Yorkshire, had commissioned the promising young local artist to paint the beautiful girl, who was just about to travel to London for her coming-out Season.

But when Helena went to London, it was as Leo's bride because she had fallen deeply in love with the artist.

Her family refused to pay Leo for his work and the portrait stayed with him and his young wife.

And they never spoke to Helena again.

Elissa looked up wistfully at the pretty smiling face and glowing dark eyes and thought that for as long as the portrait existed, a little bit of her Mama would always be alive in the world.

"Lovely, weren't she, miss?" Kitty smiled, coming into the room and placing a piping hot cup of tea on the little table next to Elissa.

"I never knew 'er, but I can just tell from the way she looks in that there picture, she was somethin' special. It don't seem right, miss, that you should lose 'er and then Mr. Valentine too."

Elissa sighed, remembering Christmas Eve, just a few weeks ago, when she had been sitting here in just the same place, staring into the red embers of the fire and Kitty had come to tell her that her Papa had died.

"I don't know 'ow I got the words out, miss, when I 'ad to come down and break the news to you."

Papa had asked Elissa to help him upstairs to his room so that so that he could take a short nap before they had supper together, as he was feeling tired and weak.

"I am so much looking forward to my Christmas Day with you, my darling daughter," he had told Elissa, as she helped him to lie down on his bed.

He had smiled at her, squeezed her hand and that was the last time she saw him alive.

When Kitty went upstairs to tell him that supper was ready, she found him lying peacefully, still smiling, so that it took her a few moments to realise that he was no longer breathing.

"Miss, it was such a shock, I don't know 'ow you bore it," she wailed.

"Sit down, a minute, Kitty, and take the weight of *your* feet."

Elissa suddenly felt that she had to tell somebody about her strange dream.

The little maid's eyes were as big as saucers as she listened to the story of her Mama, all dressed in white and the book with the date written in it.

"Oh, miss, you must have them powers!"

"Whatever do you mean?"

"My great-auntie Gertrude, she 'ad them all right. She always knew when somethin' real bad was a-goin' to 'appen."

Elissa laughed.

"Oh Kitty, I'm sure it was just a one-off event! Perhaps – I don't know – Mama looked down from Heaven and thought she would help me face Papa's death."

Kitty shook her head and looked doubtful.

"And it wasn't something bad, Kitty, my Papa died happy and peaceful in his own home, looking forward to Christmas Day. And maybe he has gone to be with Mama, which will make them both very happy."

"And what about you, Miss Elissa?"

Elissa felt a little chill of fear run through her.

What about her?

Where could she go when the house was let out to strangers and she had no home any more?

"Everything will be fine, Kitty. Mama told me in the dream that there was a great happiness coming to me."

"Miss – you could always come back to our 'ouse with me when we 'ave to leave – you'd 'ave to share a bed with our Susan in the little box room, but my Ma wouldn't turn you away, if you 'ad nowhere else to go."

"Kitty – you are *too* kind!"

Elissa smiled at the thought of having to squash into the tiny house in Mile End with all of Kitty's brothers and sisters.

"But I am sure it will not come to that. And now I suppose we must get on with our work or we will never be ready for the prospective tenants who are coming to look at the house."

There was so much to do, she realised, as she went into the hall and took down her Papa's old fur hat from the hat stand.

So much to sort out, to be sold or given away.

She had left all his things just as they were up until now and she could not bear to think of anyone else wearing his hat.

As she stood there a shadow darkened the glass in the front door and the letterbox rattled.

The afternoon post had come.

There was just one envelope lying on the doormat.

Elissa bent to pick it up. It was addressed to her in an unfamiliar spidery handwriting.

She opened it, took out the letter inside and read it,

"Fellbrook Towers, Fellbrook, Yorkshire

17th January, 1903

Dear Elissa,

It has come to my attention that you have recently suffered an unfortunate bereavement. I assume that your wastrel of a father will not have made any provision for your future, and I should like to offer you a roof over your head and such meals as are necessary in exchange for your services as a companion.

I am old and infirm and am in need of someone to run errands and help me with my day-to-day affairs.

You will not know who I am, but I am the mother of Helena Hartwell, your mother. I would not like to see my granddaughter suffer unduly for the foolishness of her silly mother, which is why I am writing to make this offer.

Unless I hear from you to the contrary, I shall send the carriage to meet the five o'clock train at Fellbrook Station on the 25th of January.

Yours,

Mabel Hartwell."

Elissa took a deep breath and tried to steady her shaking hands.

Her grandmother had written to her!

And wanted to offer her a home!

She looked down at the letter again.

Something about those cold words and the angular spiky handwriting made her feel uncomfortable, as if the writer was perhaps not such a pleasant person.

But – what choice did Elissa have?

And had not her Mama told her in her dream that there was great happiness coming to her?

Perhaps it might have something to do with this letter.

"Kitty!" Elissa called out. "I have something else to tell you!"

And in spite of her sadness, she could not help but feel excited at the thought of the journey she must make in just a few days' time and her mysterious grandmother who would be waiting for her at the end of it.

CHAPTER TWO

There was a commotion in Lanchberry Close.

Richard could hear men's voices and a thumping noise like someone beating a clenched fist against a door.

He pulled the covers over his head hoping that the noise would go away.

It was not quite nine o'clock and since his return to England several days ago, he had not felt much like getting out of bed before noon.

Each morning Travis brought him a tray of tea and toast to his bedroom and then just left him in peace.

But all the noise did not go away and when Travis politely knocked at the bedroom door and entered, the old butler was not carrying a tray and told him apprehensively,

"There be some gentlemen asking to see you, Mr. Richard. I told them that you are not at home, but they are very persistent."

Richard rolled over in bed and sat up.

"What – you mean all that noise is outside our front door?"

"Yes indeed, Mr. Richard, and I have asked them to leave several times, but they will not go."

"Then I suppose I had better go and speak to them," sighed Richard.

He climbed out of bed and wrapped himself in his father's old velvet dressing gown, which he had taken to wearing. The faint scent of Sir Julius's cigars still clung to it, which was very comforting.

As soon as the front door opened, a large gentleman in a long black coat placed his foot on the threshold.

"Mr. Richard Stanfield?" he blustered. "Boustred of Boustred and Sons, Gentleman's Outfitters."

Richard wished that he had taken the time to dress properly, but it was too late now.

"And good morning to you, Mr. Boustred. Won't you come in?"

The large gentleman, accompanied by two others, also in black coats, followed him into the drawing room.

"I would suppose you have come about the bill for my suits – " began Richard.

Mr. Boustred cleared his throat.

"I am afraid it is a little more serious than that, Mr. Stanfield. We have a number of accounts that have not been settled, both from you and Sir Julius. I believe that even the fine dressing gown you are wearing this morning has not yet been paid for."

"It was my Papa's. He has passed away – "

"Indeed so. We are more than aware of the difficult circumstances and we have been most lenient up until this time, as we were certain that you would contact us at your convenience to make appropriate payment."

"Of course. How much do you want?"

The words stuck in his throat as he could only think about his overdrawn bank account and the few coins in his pockets that were all that remained of the fortune he had inherited.

"The total outstanding is three hundred pounds, Mr. Stanfield."

Richard caught his breath with shock.

Poor Sir Julius would be turning in his grave as he had always paid his accounts on time.

"I don't think I am going to be able to lay my hands on such a large sum right now," he responded.

"Then I have to advise you, Mr. Stanfield, that we shall have to contact our Solicitors and you will soon find that you not only have us to pay, but also them!"

Mr. Boustred was eyeing him in a most unpleasant fashion.

"You can have the dressing gown back if you like."

The gentleman's outfitter snorted.

Clearly he was not in the mood for a joke.

"All right – I will see what can be done and I will get back to you next week," added Richard.

Mr. Boustred shook his head wearily.

"I wouldn't do it for anyone else," he said. "But Sir Julius was a good customer and a true gentleman. I will give you until Tuesday to settle the account."

He paused and looked around the drawing room.

"I'm no expert, but it looks like there's a good few thousand pounds worth of stuff hanging on these walls."

And with that he and his two colleagues strode out of the drawing room.

Richard sat down on the sofa to recover himself.

Mr. Boustred was right.

The paintings that Sir Julius had collected over his lifetime and had loved so much could be sold and would probably fetch a good sum of money.

It was just that he could not bear to take them down from the walls and sell them.

Travis then entered with the breakfast tray and laid it beside him.

He coughed politely.

"What is it, Travis?"

"There is the small matter of the servants' wages, Mr. Richard. As you know, Sir Julius paid us annually on the first of January each year. The money is only a couple of weeks late, but anxieties have been expressed – "

Richard held his head in his hands for a moment.

This was the last straw.

He had to face up to what must be done.

He was never going to get back the money he had lost in Argentina.

No. 13 Lanchberry Close and all its contents must be sold, the debts must be paid and somehow, he, Richard Stanfield, must begin a new life.

A life that would be very different from anything he had known so far.

*

"I really don't know what I can do with all Papa's clothes," Elissa sighed, as she looked at the pile of coats, trousers and colourful jackets that she had just cleared out of the wardrobe in his bedroom.

"And what about all the things in the studio? The oil paints and his brushes and – "

"There sure be a lot of stuff," muttered Kitty. "Far too much to carry with you, miss."

"Exactly. But how am I going to get rid of it all? Who would want a grubby old painter's smock with all the colours of the rainbow splashed all over it? Only me – for all the happy memories."

"Miss Elissa – you could always leave everything 'ere. We could 'ide it all in the loft."

"Oh Kitty, and what about the new people who will move in?"

"No one ever goes up in a loft, miss. Only to dump the stuff they ain't got no use for any more. We tuck all your father's things away in a corner up there. No one will ever know."

"Kitty – you are a genius!"

"And then maybe one day, when you be a rich lady, miss, you can come back and claim it all."

"Do you really think that might happen?"

"But your Mama said that you 'ad great 'appiness comin' to you, didn't she, miss? *In your dream*?"

"Yes, she did, Kitty. But it might take a while to happen! Come on, let's get everything packed up."

Elissa felt glad that she did not have to throw away her Papa's possessions. She liked the idea of them being safely hidden away in a secret corner of the house where he had lived and worked for so many years.

Once that was completed, there was just one more difficult task to face.

Mr. Gabriel Harker, an art dealer from Bond Street, was coming to take all her father's paintings away.

A tall upright man in an elegantly-cut tweed suit, Mr. Harker did not have much good news for Elissa.

"I admire your father's work," he said. "He is sadly neglected and not appreciated as he deserves to be. I'll try and find a buyer or two to take some of them. But I can't promise anything."

Then he offered to take all the paintings and keep them in his warehouse.

"At least you will know that the pictures are safe and being properly stored. And – who knows, perhaps one day tastes will change," he told Elissa.

She agreed, because what else could she do?

She certainly could not take all the big canvasses to Yorkshire with her. But seeing them packed up in brown paper and cardboard and carried out of the house was like losing the last little bit of her beloved Papa.

She was so upset that she quite forgot to give Mr. Harker the address of her new home in Yorkshire.

*

"So Mr. Stanfield. Shall I run through these figures again for you?"

The lawyer peered at Richard over the top of his glasses.

"I think I have understood, Mr. Grey."

Richard had no head for figures himself and he did not think that another lengthy explanation of what sums of money were owing, and how they could now be paid off, would be of any use to him.

A buyer had been found for the house and this man had agreed to purchase all the furniture and fittings as well.

The proceeds from the sale would pay off the debts. It would also pay what was owing to the servants, and give them a little bit extra to tide them over until they could find new situations.

As far as Richard was concerned, that was all he needed to know.

"I must say, it seems no time at all since we sat here at this very same table to discuss your inheritance after the sad demise of your father," said Mr. Grey, fixing Richard with his sharp little eyes. "And now what very different circumstances we find ourselves in today."

He was clearly curious to know what Richard had done with the fortune that Sir Julius had left him.

But Richard had no intention of confiding in him the details of what had happened.

All that was private, personal and *most* painful.

He rose from the table.

"Thank you so much, Mr. Grey. If you will now proceed with everything as we discussed."

The lawyer stood up too and shuffled all the papers together.

"If I can be of any further assistance – "

"Then I shall certainly contact you," said Richard, politely and waited for Mr. Grey to leave.

It was very strange to think that soon he would be without a roof over his head, but at least from now on he would not have to face any more furious Mr. Boustreds threatening to take him to Court.

Travis was hovering in the doorway.

"Mr. Richard, there is another gentleman here. I have told him that you will be settling all your accounts over the next few days, but he insists on speaking to you."

The old butler was looking grey and tired.

There had been so many comings and goings to the house over the last few days and so many angry creditors banging at the door that Travis was rushed off his feet.

"Let him wait a moment, Travis," replied Richard. "I – just want to say that I am very sorry about all of this. It has been so hard for you. And – have you found another situation?"

Travis had served Sir Julius for more than twenty years since before Richard was born.

Now the old man smiled.

"No, Mr. Richard. I will be hanging up my butler's apron and going to my sister's in Norfolk. I shall be very comfortable there, I'm sure."

"Well, that is good news, Travis!"

Richard felt suddenly lighter as he saw that the old man was genuinely pleased to be retiring.

"Papa would be so pleased to know that all is well with you. But – who is this man at the door?"

"A Mr. Jones, sir, from the bank."

"Oh, show him in! He will be very pleased to hear what I have to tell him."

Mr. Jones, a small man with watery blue eyes, was indeed happy to hear that the overdraft would very shortly be cleared and all the creditors paid off.

"But then what of yourself, Mr. Stanfield? What are your plans for the future? There will not be much money left for you."

"I still have my father's art collection to sell."

Mr. Jones eyes darted around the room, looking at all the pictures on the walls.

"French stuff, is it?" he asked.

"Yes, some of it. There's a Monet and that picture of the Thames is a Whistler."

"Ah, then I've heard of *him*," Mr. Jones exclaimed, looking relieved. "And those two are pretty, aren't they?"

He pointed at a pair of small paintings hanging near the window.

Richard had bought them for his father's birthday, the year before he became ill.

The first painting showed a cherry tree covered in blossom with a girl in a white dress standing beneath.

And in the second the tree was covered in fruit and a young woman with long fair hair and a basket over her arm was reaching up to pick the cherries.

"They're by an English painter," he told Mr. Jones. "Leo Valentine."

Richard had always loved these two pictures.

He recalled how he had visited the artist's house to buy them and had met Mr. Valentine, a tall man with a lion-like mane of golden hair.

"Ah, yes. An English artist, very good, very good," Mr. Jones wittered on. Clearly he did not know very much about art.

"Now then – Mr. Stanfield, once you have sold the paintings may I suggest that we invest the money for you? And tie it up so that it cannot be spent? It will provide you with a small income."

"Yes," agreed Richard, "that would be a good idea, Mr. Jones. Thanks for the advice."

He then rose to show the banker to the door before the man could start asking awkward questions about what had happened in Argentina.

Once Mr. Jones had gone, Richard went up to his bedroom and pulled out his battered leather valise that he had brought back from South America.

It contained many painful memories, he reflected, as he opened it up.

Inside there was a box of watercolour paints, some brushes and a bundle of sketches and paintings.

Richard's plan, as he travelled abroad, had been to paint the exotic plants, birds and animals he came across.

He had always loved painting, but then it was not considered particularly suitable for any young gentleman to take up as a career.

When his father died, however, there was no one to criticise his decision to charge off to the tropics for a few months and absorb himself in charcoal and paint and thick velvety paper.

If only he had been able to stick to his plan!

Reluctantly he unrolled the bundle of his paintings.

There were several rough sketches of orchids and tropical ferns.

The rest were portraits of a lovely young woman.

Mercedes de Rosario.

He had never considered himself to be that good at portraiture, but as soon as he met Mercedes, he longed to capture her incredible beauty on paper.

With her glowing golden skin, her shining dark red hair and luscious black eyes, she outshone all the brilliant flowers in the tropical gardens around her mother's house in Buenos Aires.

He now looked into her laughing eyes as he held up one of the portraits.

He remembered the day he had painted it and how when it was finished, she had promised to marry him.

He could still feel the warmth of her lips against his as they kissed in the green shade of the tall trees growing in her garden, for once forgetting the watchful eyes of her mother, who always seemed to be spying on them.

That was the happiest day of his life.

He had found love and would be spending the rest of his life with the most beautiful woman he had ever known.

The sadness of losing his Papa began to recede and grow less hurtful.

Mercedes had seemed happy too for a little while. She was longing to travel to England and see all the sights of London.

But then she started to question Richard about how much he loved her.

"Do you care for me, Richard? I am afraid that you are just playing with me – I am a poor Argentinian señorita – I do not have the Paris clothes, all the pretty things that the English ladies have – "

She told him she was afraid that he was ashamed of her and her Mama, who spoke no English, and that he did not really want to take them back to London with him.

Richard gave her money to buy clothes and wrote cheques to her so that she should have some money of her own.

But however often he did so, always telling her she was the love of his life and that of course he was proud of her, she still seemed fearful and anxious.

Then one day she came to Richard and asked him to lend her a very large sum of money.

"Please, Richard, my darling! If you love me – "

Richard was ashamed to feel a little nervous about giving it to her.

But she insisted.

"It is for my family, Richard. My uncles and my brothers are involved with so many exciting new projects in our country, but they will all fail if we do not have this money, and if we succeed – then we will be rich forever. You must lend it to me, darling! *Please!*"

So he started writing a cheque for her.

"How much exactly, did you say, Mercedes?"

"Oh, my darling. I am not sure. I can't remember – I will fill it in later!"

Sir Julius had always advised Richard never to give anybody a blank cheque.

"You're just asking for trouble, young 'un, if you do that," he used to say.

But Mercedes was standing behind Richard with her arms around his neck, kissing the top of his head as he wrote out the cheque with her name on it and he simply could not say 'no' to her.

The next day, when he went to visit her, the house was closed and the blinds were drawn over the windows.

Perhaps Mercedes and her mother had gone away to sort out the family businesses she had told him about.

But three days later she had still not returned and when Richard enquired at the house nearby, an old woman informed him that Señorita de Rosario had gone away to the Pampas in the South.

"Is that where her family are? The de Rosarios?"

"Her family? Señorita de Rosario has no family," the woman told him. "They are all dead."

Richard shook his head.

What about Mercedes's mother!

That large silent woman with black hair and eyes was always watching over her. He remembered how she had watched him and every time he came to visit, her deep black eyes staring at him from under her dark brows.

But, he had never had a proper conversation with the woman.

Mercedes was always drawing him away into the garden.

Maybe she was not really Mercedes's mother.

Could it be that the beautiful girl had lied to him?

Richard then ran straight into the bank in the town and sent a wire to stop the cheque he had written.

But it was too late.

It had been cashed and for a great deal more than the amount that Mercedes had asked him to lend her.

All his money was gone. The account was empty.

Now, as he stood in the bedroom which had always been his and which now he would have to leave forever, Richard stuffed the portraits of the beautiful red-haired girl back into the valise.

It was all history now, it was over, and there was nothing he could do about it.

He had tried to find Mercedes, had travelled back and forth through the plains and mountains of Argentina, but no one knew of her. Or of the mysterious woman she had called her mother.

He had confronted the bank, who were apologetic, and said they would look into the matter, but they advised him that since his signature was on the cheque and since he had already been making regular payments to this woman, it was unlikely that they could do anything to help.

Richard picked up the brushes and the paint box.

He was about to pack them away, but something stopped him.

'I am free now,' he thought. 'I will have a small income, if I invest the money wisely from the sale of the paintings.'

Why should he now not try his hand at becoming an artist? As a profession, and not just a hobby? He could travel around England and paint landscapes, which he had always been good at.

For the first time since his return from Argentina, Richard felt a little rush of happiness.

And then he suddenly remembered Leo Valentine, the big blustering man with the mane of golden hair and a long beard – the artist who had painted the two cherry tree pictures he had bought for his father's birthday.

'I will go and see him again,' Richard decided. 'I liked him, he was wild and jolly and happy. He'll give me some good advice about being a painter.'

*

The small white house in St. John's Wood had been cleaned from the attic to the basement and white sheets had been placed over all the furniture and the walls were now empty of pictures.

Elissa was sitting by the empty fireplace wearing her coat and gloves to keep warm.

Her bag was packed and she was ready to leave for King's Cross Station to catch the train up to Yorkshire.

There was a loud knock at the front door.

'That will be the House Agent come to collect the keys,' Elissa reckoned, as she jumped up to answer it.

But when she opened the door, a young man stood there. Tall and strong with wavy black hair and vivid blue eyes that were gazing straight into hers.

"Oh, goodness!" he exclaimed. "Hello!"

Elissa felt her heart beating fast.

He was smiling at her, and his whole being seemed so vibrant and alive she did not know what to say to him.

She realised that it was a very long time since she had spoken to a young man.

She had spent so many days with her ailing father, and then all the men who had come to talk to her about the letting of the house seemed old, dull and preoccupied.

None of them looked at her as this young man was doing now.

"I've come to see Leo – Leo Valentine, the artist," the young man was saying.

"I'm sorry – but my Papa has passed away," Elissa managed to reply, her voice feeling thick and tight.

"Oh, no!"

The young man's face fell.

"How awful! I so wanted to speak to him – "

And then he blushed.

"I mean, how awful for *you* – I'm so sorry – Miss Valentine."

"I am just about to leave," said Elissa, taking pity on him, "but why don't you come in for a few moments? The House Agent will be here soon, but I could make you a cup of tea."

The young man followed her into the drawing room gazing around at the dark outlines on the bare walls, which showed where pictures had once hung.

"We are in the same boat," he said. "I am Richard, by the way. Richard Stanfield. I have just had to clear out *our* house and sell up."

He held out his hand and took Elissa's and even through her glove she could feel how warm his touch was.

"My Papa died, too, not so long ago. It's hard, isn't it?" he breathed.

Elissa did not trust herself to speak, but she nodded.

"Oh, goodness – your hair!" he exclaimed. "Your lovely golden hair! You must be the girl in the pictures of the cherry tree!"

Elissa nodded again and managed to blurt out,

"I would expect so. I was always here – and Papa often painted me."

"And what will you do now?"

Richard was holding her hand tightly.

"Do you have somewhere to go?"

"I am going to stay with my grandmother."

There was a loud rap at the door.

"I imagine that will be the House Agent," he said. "No time for tea, then!"

Elissa shook her head.

"I'm going off to be a painter," Richard was saying. "That is why I wanted to talk to your father, but – Miss Valentine – it's been wonderful to see you. I'm sure we'll meet again sometime."

"Yes," Elissa whispered.

It was all too much suddenly, this handsome young man was being so kind to her. And all the while she knew that in just a few minutes she would be walking out of the front door of her home perhaps for ever.

"I do hope so!" responded Richard enthusiastically, smiling at her.

Then he let go of her hand and was gone.

It was time for Elissa to leave too.

She picked up the keys and went to hand them over to the House Agent.

CHAPTER THREE

It was growing dark by the time the train drew into Fellbrook Station at five o'clock, and Elissa peered along the dimly-lit platform to see if anyone had come to meet her.

"How do, lass!" a deep gruff voice spoke up from the shadows. "Miss Valentine, is it?"

"Yes, that's me!" acknowledged Elissa and as she spoke her breath formed a misty cloud in the cold air.

"Oldroyd it be, ma'am, coachman at The Towers," the gruff voice came again and a squat man with broad shoulders stepped forward to pick up her bag.

He raised his hat and indicated for Elissa to follow him along the platform to where a carriage pulled by four horses was waiting.

"Is it far?" asked Elissa, as the coachman opened the door.

"Far enough," grunted Oldroyd.

And then she was inside the carriage, sitting on soft leather cushions with her bag at her feet.

The carriage rattled and jolted as the horses swiftly trotted along the road and then it slowed down and Elissa realised they were climbing up a steep incline.

She pulled down the window to look out and a blast of bitterly cold air rushed into the carriage.

On the seat opposite lay a heavy fur rug and Elissa picked it up and wrapped it round her shoulders.

It felt soft and luxurious and, as she snuggled into its warm folds, a strong perfume of violets tickled her nose.

Outside a full moon was rising in the velvety dark sky and its silvery light shone over a barren hillside with just a few stunted trees dotted about.

She listened to the four horses' hooves slipping and scraping as they pulled the carriage up the steep road, and every now and then Oldroyd shouted at them and clicked his tongue to hurry them along.

In spite of the warm fur Elissa felt cold inside.

Where were they going?

There were no buildings or lights anywhere on the hillside and she felt as if she was on her way to the end of the world.

The icy air drifting in through the window smelt of moorland herbs and wet marshland. Elissa had never smelt anything quite so clean and wild and fresh before.

Then she caught a more familiar scent – the tang of wood smoke.

There must be a house nearby, a farmhouse perhaps where there was a fire burning.

Elissa leaned her head out of the carriage window and caught her breath in astonishment when she saw what lay ahead.

It was no farmhouse.

A mass of dark battlemented towers crowned the brow of the hill and she might almost have thought that the carriage was taking her towards a huge Castle, except for the lights that shone out from the tall windows at the front of the building.

'Of course,' she whispered, 'Grandmama's address is Fellbrook Towers – and that must be what I can see.'

The carriage lurched up the last slope and came to a grinding halt.

Oldroyd came to open the door for Elissa.

"Fellbrook Towers, miss," he announced proudly.

The moon was now high and casting its silver light over the many roofs of The Towers, but as Elissa walked up to the huge front door, she felt as if she was stepping into a deep shadow.

'I cannot stay here!' she sighed, her heart fluttering in panic, as the great old door creaked in front of her and opened up a crack. 'This is not my home!'

And she then turned to run back to the carriage, but Oldroyd was already leading the horses away towards the stables.

An eye was peering through the crack and after a moment a woman's voice with a strong Yorkshire accent muttered,

"It be 'er, my Lady!"

The door then swung fully open to let Elissa inside.

The hall that she walked into was vast and gloomy, its vaulted ceiling so high above her head it was invisible in the darkness. It felt almost as big as the Railway Station at King's Cross, where she had boarded the train that very morning.

Ahead of her to the right a staircase wide enough to drive a coach up it led up towards a balustraded landing.

And to the left in a huge fireplace a blazing fire was burning.

In front of the fire a woman was standing, but the flames were so bright that Elissa could only make out her silhouette.

She was very tall with hair piled on top of her head.

"Nantwich!" the woman called and her strong bell-like voice echoed around the hall. "Bring her to me!"

The stout housekeeper, who had opened the front door, now bustled forward and took Elissa's bag.

"Go on, then," she hissed. "Her Ladyship is waitin' for you, can't you see?"

Elissa approached the crackling fire, and now she could see the flickering flames reflected in the woman's dark eyes, making sparkles in the cascades of jet beads that hung from her ears.

She stood there as straight and upright as a much younger woman, but the skin on her aristocratic fine-boned face was lined and drooping, although her elegant coiffure showed very few traces of grey.

Elissa noticed a strong scent of violets – the same perfume that had clung to the fur rug in the carriage.

"So you have come," the woman said after a while. "But I cannot see your face. Take off your hat."

Elissa drew out her hatpins and removed the straw hat she had worn for the journey.

Her heavy fair hair, which she had tied in a knot at the back of her neck, fell down over her shoulders.

The woman made an odd noise somewhere between a hiss and sigh.

"So – you are *Elissa*, are you?

"Yes, I am. And you must be – Lady Hartwell, my Grandmama."

Elissa moved to step closer, but the woman raised a hand to stop her.

"That is so. Although now that I see you in front of me, I find it hard to believe that we could be related. I see nothing of our family in your face – and your *hair* – "

"I take after my Papa! My hair is the same colour as his."

"No!"

Lady Hartwell's voice echoed off the walls of the vast hall.

"I will not have you refer to that man whilst you are under my roof!"

Elissa was so shocked and confused that she did not know what to say.

"We Hartwells are dark-haired, all of us. It is a vast disappointment to me to see that you have not inherited my daughter Helena's beauty."

Lady Hartwell turned away to stare into the fire.

"Grandmama – " Elissa began, struggling to collect her thoughts.

"No!" the old woman snorted. "You do *not* call me that. *Lady Hartwell* is my title."

Her black eyes flashed in the light from the fire and Elissa could see just how striking she must have been as a young woman.

"I am sorry, Lady Hartwell. I was just going to say that mother was indeed very beautiful – "

Elissa thought Lady Hartwell might be pleased if she went on to say that she must have passed on her good looks to her mother, but the old woman was not listening.

She was staring beyond Elissa into the shadows at the far end of the hall, her eyes fixed on some scene from the past.

"She was the most beautiful girl in London Society. She could have taken her pick of all the young aristocrats that Season and yet she chose to throw herself away on an ignorant and worthless young portrait painter!"

Lady Hartwell's voice dropped dramatically as she spat out the words.

"She broke my heart, the cruel thoughtless hussy!"

Elissa could not think of anyone less heartless and unkind than her dear Mama, who had been so sensitive and loving. But it did not seem a good idea to contradict Lady Hartwell, whose thin black eyebrows were now lowered in a fierce frown.

So she simply added,

"My mother spoke of you often and said that she missed you."

Lady Hartwell tossed her head and the jet earrings tinkled as the beads clicked together.

"That is as it may be. Helena made her choice and she suffered the consequences!"

She turned from Elissa to speak to the housekeeper.

"Nantwich, I feel rather disinclined to take dinner this evening."

And with that she strode towards the wide staircase, the endless layers of her black satin skirts rustling over the flagstones and leaving behind them a faint flowery scent of violets.

Elissa watched Lady Hartwell's aristocratic figure ascending until it merged into the darkness of the balcony and disappeared.

"If you would care to come with me, miss."

They walked along a purple-carpeted corridor and then the housekeeper opened up a panelled door and Elissa could see a long dining table, which stretched away in front of her like a broad river of polished wood.

At the far end of the table, a blaze of candlelight was reflected in its shining surface, and here two places were laid with gold-rimmed plates, delicate glasses and an array of knives, forks and spoons.

"There you be, miss, and I shall now tell cook you are at table. We mustn't keep the food waiting."

She then walked away down the dining room and disappeared through another door.

No one seemed to have thought that Elissa might like to change or brush her hair or even wash her hands.

She looked at the place opposite and tried to picture Lady Hartwell seated there.

The old lady was fierce and rather frightening, but Elissa would almost have preferred her company now to the total silence of the deserted dining room.

She could feel her eyes begin to sting as a wave of sadness welled up inside her.

'I must not, I will not cry!' she told herself firmly and closed her eyes tightly to hold back the tears.

Behind her closed lids she could see the winter sun shining over St. John's Wood that morning and the face of the handsome young man who had knocked at the door.

Where was he now?

Something nudged against her foot and Elissa gave a little scream and leapt up – someone had come into the dining room and sat down in front of her.

She opened her eyes, but the chair opposite her was empty, its red velvet cushion glowing in the candlelight.

'Something – *touched* me – ' Elissa whispered to herself. But perhaps it was her imagination playing tricks on her.

She looked around her, but there was nothing to be seen beyond the bright glow of the candles except a veil of shadows masking the dining room walls.

Then a door creaked open and a butler in black and flanked by two footmen, came slowly towards her, bearing an immense silver tureen.

Elissa sat down again still shaking from shock and hoped they had not heard her scream.

"Soup, miss?"

The butler, who sported long mutton-chop whiskers came and stood beside her.

Elissa nodded, hiding her trembling hands beneath the white linen tablecloth.

One of the footmen lifted the lid of the tureen and the other passed a silver ladle to the butler, who dipped it into the tureen and poured a small amount of brown liquid into Elissa's soup bowl.

She was too shaken and too tired to feel hungry, but when she raised a spoonful of the soup to her lips, it tasted delicious.

Within a few moments the butler was bearing down upon her again, this time with a large silver platter.

He had just about reached her chair when she felt something brush against her leg again.

"Oh!" Elissa gasped and she would have jumped up again if the butler had not been stooping over her shoulder to serve the next course.

"Is something wrong, miss?" the butler asked her, sliding a piece of something drowned in a white sauce onto her plate.

"Nothing, it's – nothing," she replied and the butler and the two footmen retreated once more.

Now a strange noise could be heard and it seemed to be coming from under the dining table.

There was something familiar and quite comforting about this odd noise and Elissa plucked up her courage and lifted the edge of the tablecloth so she could peep under.

A pair of wide green eyes gazed up at her from the darkness.

"Oh my goodness, what are you doing there?" she whispered, as a fat ginger cat stood up and rubbed against her leg. "Oh, but it's the fish course – and I expect that is your favourite."

Quickly before the butler and the footmen returned, she broke off a piece of fish and passed it down to the cat. And then another and another until all of the fish had gone.

Through the rest of that long and lonely dinner, as the butler and the two footmen went back and forth with a succession of dishes for which she had no appetite, the cat kept her company, lying on her feet and purring softly.

Later that night when Elissa was lying wide awake in her luxurious bedroom, watching the moon travel slowly across the sky through the half-open curtains, she heard a scratching noise at her door.

"Hello!" she called out, as she opened the door and the ginger cat slipped into the room and jumped onto her bed.

"So you found me up here too! What's your name, puss? It should be 'Marmalade' as that is what you look like with your broad orange and red stripes! You are the brightest thing I have seen here so far at The Towers where everything seems to be black or grey or purple!"

The cat curled up at the foot of her four-poster bed and started purring loudly.

'*I have a friend*,' mused Elissa as she laid her head on the pillow and within moments she was fast asleep.

*

"Richard, you are many miles away!" Montgomery Milward said, punching his best friend on the arm. "Wake up, man!"

They were strolling along Regent's Street towards Piccadilly and high up in the sky above the same moon that peeped in on Elissa in her new home was shining down on them.

"Sorry, Monty."

"It's your last night out in London, old chap! I'm taking time out from my legal studies to wine you and dine you and delight your eyes with some of the prettiest girls on the London stage – you might at least look like you're enjoying yourself."

"I am Monty, I am – "

"Just look on the bright side, Richard. You are now a free man, no ties to bind you and you're going off to do what you've always wanted, trying your hand at painting."

"Yes."

Monty was right, he should be delighted.

He might have lost almost everything, but at least he had the opportunity to start a new life, doing something he loved.

"Oh, no!" Monty groaned and struck his forehead. "Don't tell me, Richard, you are still mooning over that wicked woman who broke your heart and cheated you out of your fortune!"

"Absolutely not," shuddered Richard.

"I know that lovesick look in your eyes – "

"No, no, no!"

"Oh – it's even worse! You have met another one, haven't you?"

Richard shook his head vigorously, but Monty was not deterred and kept on pestering him until he was forced to admit it, that yes, he had met a beautiful young girl that very morning.

"Honestly, Richard, I can't let you out of my sight! It's a good job that I'll be at the theatre with you tonight or you'd be running off with some silly actress."

"This girl was – different, Monty."

"Aren't they all?" replied Monty with a cynical air.

Richard did not respond and Monty, seeing that he had upset his friend, continued,

"All right then, old man. Spill the beans. What is she like?"

"She has fair hair," began Richard, seeing Elissa in his mind's eye, answering the door with her long golden curls falling over the shoulders of her old black dress.

"Fair. Well, that's a good start. If you'd said she was a redhead like that girl from Argentina, I would have been very worried. She's *very* rich, I hope?"

"She's an artist's daughter."

"Hmm." Monty looked a bit doubtful. "Is her Papa famous?"

"He is dead. And he was not very well known."

"*Richaaard*!" growled Monty, striking his forehead again. "You need a girl with a fortune, if you're going to be a struggling painter!"

"But she – "

"Was very pretty, I'd expect!" interrupted Monty. "Stay away from her, Richard. Find yourself a nice little heiress!"

"I'll probably never see her again, Monty. She's leaving London and I am such a fool, I didn't think to ask her where she was going."

Monty gave a sigh of relief and took his arm.

"Thank goodness for that, Richard. Come on, let's crack open a bottle of champagne!"

And he gently steered Richard towards the lighted windows of one of Piccadilly's finest restaurants.

If his old friend was going to be wandering all over the country, sitting out in all weathers painting mountains and ruins and staying in uncomfortable local inns, Monty was determined that his last night in London should be one to remember.

But even several bottles of champagne and a bevy of pretty dancers who all flirted with him madly, could not erase Elissa's lovely face from Richard's mind.

He would see her again.

He *had* to see her again.

She would come back into his life he was sure.

*

It was eleven o'clock in the morning and the sun was streaming in through the windows of Lady Hartwell's parlour.

Elissa had been sitting there for a couple of hours in this stuffy room waiting for her Grandmama, who seemed to be taking a long time to rise from her bed.

A fat white pug dog was patrolling the parlour on bandy little legs and Elissa held her hand out to it, but it growled at her and backed away.

Then it barked loudly and ran to the door as Lady Hartwell dressed in purple velvet swept into the room.

Elissa jumped to her feet.

Her grandmother frowned at her with an expression of extreme disapproval.

"That dress is a disgrace," she said in her loud clear voice. "The least of my parlour maids would be instantly dismissed if I found her in such a garment."

"I am sorry, but this is the only black dress I have."

"Such an unsuitable colour!"

"I am in mourning for my father."

The old woman sniffed haughtily.

"Duties of remembrance to that unspeakable man have surely been carried out by now!"

"But Papa has been dead only a few weeks."

Elissa was determined to stand her ground and she raised her eyes to meet the old woman's fierce dark gaze.

"*Well.* If you insist on prolonging this nonsense, I shall ask Mrs. Nantwich to look out a spare black gown for you from the servants' outfits. And your hair is hanging round your face like a schoolgirl's. Did you not bring your maid with you to dress it?"

"I don't have a maid. I have always done my own hair."

Lady Hartwell sniffed.

"I suppose then it falls to me to provide you with a maid. I simply cannot endure to have you looking such a fright. Ring the bell! I now require a cup of hot chocolate immediately."

Elissa looked around her for a bell, but could see nothing that resembled one.

Then she realised that there was a long embroidered panel of material hanging by the fireplace with a tassel on the end of it.

She walked to it, pulled it cautiously and a distant peal sounded from somewhere below.

Lady Hartwell sat down on the sofa in front of the fire and the little dog ran barking up to her.

"Get away, Nelson," the old woman said, pushing the little creature away with her foot. "I have a dreadful headache and I really cannot be bothered with you now."

Elissa wondered what she should do now.

She felt like the dog, for her grandmother obviously could not be bothered with her either. She had been rude about Elissa's appearance and now she was ignoring her completely.

"Lady Hartwell, would you like me to take the pug outside for a walk?" she asked.

The old woman's fierce black eyes stared at her in surprise.

"A walk? Whatever for? Nelson is a lap dog. He stays with me in the parlour."

"I just thought that perhaps his barking might make your head feel worse – "

Lady Hartwell frowned and put her fingers to her temples.

"Go on then, you take him! At least I won't have to suffer the sight of you looking so disreputable. Make sure that you bring him back safely."

"Of course, Lady Hartwell."

The pug growled at Elissa and ran under the sofa, hiding behind his Mistress's purple skirts.

"Whatever are you doing, grovelling on the floor in that ridiculous way?" asked Lady Hartwell, as Elissa went down on all fours and tried to catch him.

She was just about to give up when a maid arrived with a heavy tray of hot chocolate, and as Nelson emerged his nose twitching at the aroma, Elissa caught him by his jewelled collar.

She slipped out of the parlour and down the wide stairs into the hall.

It looked so different in daylight and she could see an array of portraits of her dark-haired Hartwell ancestors gazing down at her from high up on the walls.

Nelson began shivering as soon as they stepped out of the front door and Elissa picked him up and held him close to her to keep him warm.

Stretching all around her was an intricate pattern of flowerbeds lined by neatly trimmed box hedges and in the distance endless bushes clipped into geometric shapes.

'Papa would have hated this garden,' she reflected. 'There are no colours, it's far too formal and nothing wild anywhere to be seen.'

The pug wriggled in her arms and Elissa put him down on the garden path and let him run about among the flowerbeds.

No wonder he was so fat if he had to stay indoors all the time in the hot stuffy parlour.

After a few minutes he trotted back to her panting and she picked up him again.

Then she looked up at the sunlight shining over the hills beyond the garden, picking up bright flashes of green and yellow.

And crossing the hill was a path leading away into the distance and looking almost golden in the bright light.

"I wonder where that leads to?" she asked the little dog. "Don't you think it looks intriguing? It's far too cold today, but we shall go there, Nelson, as soon as we can."

And a thrill of excitement passed through her body as she spoke.

However tough life at Fellbrook Towers might be, the hills and moors beyond the house were full of beauty and promise just waiting to be discovered.

CHAPTER FOUR

Richard squeezed a little more yellow from the tube of paint onto his palette.

He was so completely lost in the thrill of his latest painting that he hardly noticed that his fingers were quite numb with cold.

The shade of green was not quite right yet – and he wanted to capture exactly the colour of the lonely Sussex Downs that rose up into the clear blue winter sky in front of him.

Once he had perfected the faded tint of the wintry grass that covered the Downs, then he could add the details of the leafless thorn trees and the shepherd's wooden hut that would bring life and interest to the picture.

"Cold work, my lad," came a voice from over his shoulder.

Richard jumped with surprise.

He had not noticed that the old shepherd who lived in the hut had come up behind him and was watching him at his work.

"Yes – it is!"

"I shall be lightin' the stove and brewin' up, young man, if you'd like to come and join me," said the shepherd, leaning on his crook as he surveyed the rough outlines on Richard's canvas.

"Thank you, but I shall need to finish this before the light goes."

"Tis a fine thing, devotion!" the shepherd muttered and patted Richard on the shoulder. "It will reap you great rewards, young sir."

He ambled off down the winding sheep track that led to his hut.

Now that he had mixed the perfect green, Richard's brush flew across the canvas filling in the gentle curves of the Downs.

A plume of smoke rose up from the chimney on the wooden hut as the shepherd now lit his stove and Richard sighed with satisfaction, as he watched it drift up into the clear sky as it would make a perfect finishing touch to his composition.

He worked swiftly away adding the trail of smoke to his canvas and as the shepherd emerged from the hut and walked back up the path, he put the old man in the painting too with few quick strokes of paint.

"'ere, young sir, this'll warm you a little," the old man said and held out a tin mug of scalding hot tea.

Richard wrapped his scarf around the mug, so it did not burn his hands and sipped the tea gratefully.

"I'm almost done. I've the colours down and that's most important as they change incredibly quickly when the sun begins to set."

"You've caught the scene to the very life!" the old shepherd exclaimed, bending down to peer at the painting. "Why – there I am, comin' up the path just now. 'ow you can do it, young sir, I dinna know!"

"I'm glad you think it looks lifelike, for you know this place better than anyone else. If I can please you, I must be doing something right! But – forgive me, I don't know your name?"

"Old Newman, they call me," he chuckled. "I shall not be offended if you laughs, sir, as most folk do!"

"I shall call this picture after you, Old Newman, in gratitude for this excellent cup of tea."

The shepherd was quite overcome at the idea.

"I didn't think to be famous in me old age!"

"Steady on!" Richard laughed. "It may not come to that! I have to find a gallery to take my paintings first!"

Old Newman shook his head.

"I'm no judge of art, young sir, but you have a rare talent in my opinion. I don't doubt you'll make your way in the world."

Richard felt very touched by the old man's faith in him. It warmed him almost as much as the hot tea.

"Thank you, Old Newman! I shall remember what you said," he told the shepherd and then he watched the old man make his way back along the track to his little hut.

Richard added a few final brushstrokes until the sun slipped behind the tall Downs and the sky began to darken. Soon the first stars would be coming out.

It was time to go.

He stretched out his stiff limbs and started to pack away his paints and brushes, trying to ignore the sadness that always fell on him when he finished work for the day, and he remembered once again that he had no home and no loved ones to care for him.

At least he could be sure of warmth and company tonight.

He was staying at a local inn, *The Stag*, and though the food was plain and the bed was narrow and hard, the landlady, Mrs. Betts, made him most welcome as she had a son the same age as Richard who was serving in the Army.

'I do hope Old Newman is right,' he mused, as he hurried down the steep lane that led to the village. '*I* don't know if I'm any good.'

He wished again that Leo Valentine was still alive to help him and give him advice.

And, as always happened when he thought of the old artist, he remembered his daughter Elissa, the lovely girl with the glorious golden hair.

Was she too feeling lonely on this icy spring night?

He knew nothing about where she had gone, when like him she had to leave her old home.

Richard opened the door of the inn and stepped into warmth and noise and then Mrs. Betts called out a cheerful greeting to him from behind the bar.

'I've been so lucky,' he thought. 'Everyone I have met since I left London has been so kind to me."

As he took off his coat and prepared to sit down to a hearty meal of Mrs. Betts' finest steak-and-kidney pie, he sent up a little prayer that Elissa, wherever she might be, and whoever she might be with, was meeting with as much kindness as he had found in this quiet corner of Sussex.

*

The wind caught at Elissa's hair and pulled it loose from her earlier unsuccessful attempt to put it up.

"Oh, Nelson, I shall be in trouble again," she sighed, as she tried to recapture it with a couple of hairpins.

The little pug barked joyfully at her and scampered away between the box hedges enjoying his freedom.

Elissa was happy to be in the open air too.

It had been a long day sitting in the stuffy parlour, winding Lady Hartwell's embroidery wool and ringing the bell endlessly for hot chocolate and smelling salts.

She stretched her arms above her head and looked out beyond the garden at the wild green hillside, where the mysterious path stretched away into the distance.

"I *must* find out where that leads soon!" she cried and the little dog heard her voice and came trotting back to her to see what she was doing.

"What would we do without our walks?" she asked him, patting his small round head.

"My Grandmama does not like me, Nelson," Elissa confided in a low voice, although there was no one in the garden to hear her.

"I look like my Papa whom she hated. And all day long I sit with her and speak politely and do everything she asks me to and yet she scarcely speaks a word to me and will not look at me at all."

She shivered at the thought that her Ladyship had finally found a maid for her, insisting that the girl should work alongside her own French maid, Ernestine, until she was fully satisfied that she was ready to take up her duties with Elissa.

The thought that from now on there would always be someone with her in her bedroom, fussing around and telling her what to do struck a chill into Elissa's heart, and made her reluctant to go back inside despite the cold wind and the darkening sky at the end of the afternoon.

What if *her* maid was like grim old Ernestine, who after many long years at The Towers was just as fierce and unsmiling as her Mistress?

But there was nothing to be done and at least Lady Hartwell's constant complaints about the state of Elissa's hair and clothes would come to an end.

Elissa had little time to fret over the thought of her new maid as Nelson suddenly leapt up and began barking.

"What is it, little one?" she enquired and then she could see beyond the garden wall that someone was riding a black horse over the hilltop towards The Towers.

"Why, well done, Nelson! Someone's coming! He is still quite far away, but you knew! Well done!"

The pug peered up at her with his bulging black eyes, grateful for her praise.

Elissa watched as the horseman drew to a halt, so swiftly that his horse reared up.

"He's coming here," she remarked to the dog. "He's stopped to look at The Towers!"

She would have liked to stay and watch as horse and rider came nearer, but a few fat drops of rain began to fall from the sky and Nelson whined unhappily and pawed at her feet.

"Let's go in then, little one. Perhaps there will be a guest at dinner tonight and I will not have to sit in silence and watch her Ladyship complain about the food."

"I'm sorry, miss, I don't mean to 'urt you," Ellen, her new young maid, exclaimed as she pulled a long comb through Elissa's long tresses just before dinner. "I'm not much used to dressin' a lady's 'air."

Ellen was not in any way the person that Elissa had expected, being young and shy and nervous on her first evening on duty.

"Please don't worry, Ellen, it is my fault if there are tangles. The wind was blowing so hard in the garden this afternoon. I should not have gone out."

"You are very kind, miss," said Ellen, wincing even more than Elissa as she caught another tangle in the teeth of the comb.

"Not at all. I am really so glad it is you that Lady Hartwell sent to me and not another Ernestine!"

"Oh, but Ernestine is just the perfect lady's maid! I shall never be as clever as she is at my duties."

Elissa laughed.

"I am sure Ernestine is the best of her kind, but I know she would pull my corset laces much too tight, and frown at me dreadfully if I went out for one of my walks!"

"There!"

Ellen pulled the comb through the last long strand of golden hair and began to pin it up into a knot at the back of Elissa's head.

"Is it as good as your maid in London used to do for you?" she asked anxiously.

"Oh Ellen – I've never had a maid at all! I used to always put my hair up myself when I thought about it and that wasn't very often."

Ellen's mouth fell open with surprise.

"But you are Lady Hartwell's granddaughter, aren't you!"

"Yes, I am. Though I think even she has difficulty believing it most of the time. But, Ellen, now I have you to help me, I'll start looking a little more as she would wish!"

Ellen fixed a final pin in Elissa's hair and brought her an embroidered wrap made from fine black silk to wear around her shoulders.

"There, miss. I found this among a pile of things her Ladyship was gettin' rid of. I do wish you 'ad a lovely silk dress to wear with it tonight, but it'll 'elp to make you look elegant."

Elissa adjusted the beautiful wrap to cover the plain black dress that Lady Hartwell had requisitioned for her granddaughter from the housekeeper.

"Perhaps, if there is a guest tonight, Grandmama will actually speak to me," commented Elissa, gazing at her unfamiliar, elegant reflection in the mirror.

"So far if she has not been indisposed and retired to her room with a headache, she has sat all through dinner without speaking a word."

"A guest, miss?" asked Ellen.

Elissa described the horseman she had seen riding towards The Towers.

"Oh, *miss*!"

Ellen was blushing a deep red.

"Already? He was not expected so soon – "

"Who do you mean, Ellen?"

The young maid was stumbling over her words.

"Miss – Lord Hartwell. Her Ladyship's grandson."

"Oh, then, he must be my cousin!"

Elissa felt a sharp thrill of excitement run through her veins as she realised that she was about to meet another relative of her mother's.

"Yes, miss. Fellbrook Towers belongs to 'im. But he doesn't like to live 'ere. He leaves it to 'er Ladyship to run the place."

"How strange that she has never spoken of him to me. What is he like?"

"Oh, miss – 'e is very 'andsome!"

Elissa laughed.

Clearly that was why Ellen was blushing so much.

"And – 'e likes to just turn up sometimes without any notice."

"How impulsive of him," said Elissa. "But perhaps that is a gentleman's prerogative."

"'er Ladyship will be very pleased, she is always so 'appy to see 'im."

It was time for Elissa to go downstairs, but before she did, she remembered to tell Ellen not to be afraid if she heard a strange scratching noise at the door.

"It will only be Marmalade," she explained. "He is

a dear cat and he likes to spend the night up here in my bedroom. I hope you don't mind?"

"It will be company, miss. For I expect you will be late comin' back, if 'is Lordship is at 'ome tonight."

And once again Elissa felt strangely excited at the prospect of meeting her cousin.

She sped down the staircase into the hall and then paused as she saw two people standing in front of the fire.

As always in the evenings, the hall was gloomy and the staircase was veiled in shadows, so they did not see her as she stood to watch them.

One, in long flowing skirts was Lady Hartwell and once again, Elissa thought how youthful she looked as she leaned towards the man who was bending to kiss her hand.

"Why must you stay away from us so long?" her grandmother was saying in a soft low tone that Elissa had never heard her use before.

"I wish you would not be always in London. Why must you spend all your time with gambling men and fancy ill-bred women?"

The man laughed and whispered something in the old woman's ear, almost as if he was her lover and not her grandson.

"Oh, my dearest, you do flatter me!" Lady Hartwell answered him. "But why must you come so unexpectedly? I should have liked to have cook prepare a special dinner for tonight."

The man laughed and kissed her hand again.

"I come only to see you, my darling. It is you that brings me back to The Towers every time."

Elissa saw that Mrs. Nantwich was hovering a few feet away from them.

Dinner must be ready and yet the couple who stood in front of the fire showed no signs of moving.

As Elissa stepped forward to join them, the man turned to look at her, his dark eyes gleaming like polished stones in the firelight.

"Who is this? You didn't tell me you had hired a new Governess, dearest," he exclaimed, "surely I am too old for such attention, but I think she would be quite pretty if she was more smartly dressed. Perhaps I might like to take some lessons from her – after all!"

Then he laughed heartily and Elissa felt a shock of confusion run through her heart because his expression, the shape of his dark brows and the way that he threw his head back, reminded her vividly of her Mama's beautiful face.

Lady Hartwell shook her head, looking flustered.

"Did I not tell you I had taken in Helena's daughter to be my companion? I am very lonely, here, dearest, for you are so often away."

The man's dark brows flew up in arcs of surprise and once again, Elissa saw her Mama's face in his.

"What? Wicked Aunt Helena's little chicken come home to roost! Well I never. Let me look at you."

He held out a hand, enticing Elissa to come to him.

"You are fooling with me, Grandmama," he said, staring into Elissa's face, "it's only a Governess after all."

"I – *am* Helena's daughter – " Elissa stammered.

"How can you be?" he said and he reached up and teased a strand of hair away from behind her ear, playing with it between his fingers.

"Look at you – how can you be one of us – you are *fair-haired*!"

"It is true," Elissa told him, wishing he was not so close to her as she could smell the tang of whisky on his breath.

"I am Lady Helena's daughter, my name is Elissa."

He dropped the strand of hair and turned to Lady Hartwell.

"Is this correct?"

"Why should I lie to you, Falcon?" the old woman replied. "I need a companion and since she is a relation, there is no need for me to pay her."

He clicked his teeth and looked at Elissa again.

"I cannot believe it," he said, and he reached for her again and pulled the silk wrap away from her shoulders, so that he could see the plain black dress beneath it.

"Her apparel is not even fit for a Governess – why, she might be a girl you have hired to do the mending."

"My Lord," Mrs. Nantwich stepped anxiously into the circle of firelight. "Dinner is served!"

"It must wait," he snapped. "I am not ready."

He spun round and walked to a small table where decanters of sherry and whisky stood, glowing richly in the light of the flickering flames.

He poured out a glass of sherry.

"Here, cousin," he called out. "Drink up. I cannot have a sad face at my table."

Elissa wanted to tell him she was still in mourning for her father and it did not seem right to drink, especially sherry, which she did not much like the taste of, but Lady Hartwell was sighing impatiently and peering at the little watch pinned to the front of her dress.

"Hurry up, Elissa. The soup will be ruined."

Elissa sipped the strong sweet sherry and almost at once felt her face grow hot and her head spun a little.

"*Elissa*," Lord Hartwell was saying to her now.

"A pretty name for my young cousin. And what an interesting childhood you must have had. For your father was an artist, was he not?"

Elissa nodded.

"Come, finish your sherry, don't keep us waiting, the excellent amontillado will soon raise your spirits and put roses in your cheeks to boot!"

Reluctantly she then took another sip of the sticky sweet stuff.

"I daresay you will have some lively tales to tell of your Bohemian life in London," he smiled at her in a way that made her feel uncomfortable and again his expression reminded her of her Mama.

"I have often wondered what my beautiful aunt got up to once she had escaped from The Towers."

"Falcon! Let us proceed to the dining room," Lady Hartwell insisted, her voice rising.

He leaned close to Elissa and whispered,

"I look forward to hearing everything about it when Grandmama is out of the way."

Then he nudged the sherry glass up to Elissa's lips, and held it there until she had sipped it all down and the glass was empty.

"There," he crowed, "that's so much better. You're quite presentable now you have some colour."

A tall vase of white flowers – lilies and camellias, stood by the fireplace, a little away from the heat.

He went over to it and pulled off one of the delicate camellias.

"I hate to see a young girl in black," he sighed. "It is a sin against beauty. I cannot spend the whole of dinner looking at such a sight. Here!"

He tucked the flower into Elissa's hair.

"Ah, that's better. A touch of loveliness to bring you to full life. Look, Grandmama, how the yellow at the centre of the flower picks up the colour of her hair! I am quite an artist myself tonight, aren't I?"

Elissa felt herself grow even warmer than she had already become from the sherry.

But her cousin had turned away and was offering his arm to Lady Hartwell, and Elissa, greatly relieved she was no longer the focus of his attention, followed behind as they walked into dinner.

She was scarcely able to touch any of the fine food that was laid before her through the long evening, for she expected every moment that young Lord Hartwell would turn to her again and started quizzing her about her life in St. John's Wood.

But aside from insisting that her glass was refilled constantly with champagne, which he insisted she drink up, he did not speak to her and all his chatter was addressed to Lady Hartwell who he talked endlessly to of his aristocratic friends in London.

So once again, it seemed Elissa must sit in silence through dinner.

But she did not mind tonight, for the fact that they both ignored her gave her the opportunity to look at him and marvel at just how much, despite his strong masculine features, he resembled her Mama.

When, unsteady on her feet and with the beginnings of a headache hovering above her eyes, she reached her bedroom, Ellen was sitting by the fire with Marmalade in her lap.

"Oh, miss. I've been thinkin' about you for every minute! Didn't you think 'im very 'andsome?"

Elissa sat down on the bed.

"I suppose so. Yes – he must be handsome. For he looks in his own way so very like my mother and she was an extremely beautiful woman."

"The Hartwells are a good-lookin' family, miss."

"I have drunk far too much champagne, would you bring me some water, Ellen?"

The little maid looked quite disappointed as if she would have liked to hear more gossip about Lord Hartwell, but she fetched a jug of water and helped Elissa into bed.

"Leave the curtains," asked Elissa, as she lay back with Marmalade on her feet.

Outside in the cold crisp night air, she could see the stars twinkling against the blackness of the sky.

'I must go out tomorrow,' she mused, 'and let the fresh air blow away this headache. And perhaps – maybe I will be able to leave the garden and climb up the hill – '

And so with the tantalising image of the green path stretching away into the horizon over the moors, she then fell deeply asleep.

CHAPTER FIVE

"I have a bad migraine coming on," Lady Hartwell sighed, as she lay on the sofa in her parlour next morning, looking very unwell. Her thin face was ashy pale.

"Why must my grandson be so restless?" she was moaning. "He has only just arrived back home and now he is away again. Why can he not stay here with me?"

"I did not realise he had left," remarked Elissa, very surprised.

"Oh, he went off before breakfast. He has gone to York to look at some racehorse which is for sale. He has no thought for my feelings whatsoever."

She continued to complain about her headache and seemed distressed and Elissa remembered something that her Mama had always done for her, when she was ill as a child.

She sent the parlour maid to bring her clean linen, cloths and lavender water and then knelt down beside her grandmother and gently sponged her forehead.

"I am sure Lord Hartwell will be home very soon," she commented as she smoothed the old woman's brow.

"Oh, do you think so?" Lady Hartwell gave a little snort of amusement. "You clearly do not know him. He is just as likely to go on to London from York, as come back here. I may not see him now for a month."

Elissa did not know what she should say to this, but she thought it seemed rude and inconsiderate of her cousin not at least to say farewell to his grandmother, if he was going to be away for such a long time.

"Lord Hartwell seems very fond of you," she said after a few moments. "I am sure he does not mean to cause you distress."

Lady Hartwell's dark eyes stared up at her.

"He is everything to me, all that's left of my family. His father, my darling son, died on a foolish jaunt to the West Indies. I told him he should not go, that the climate would not agree with him, but he would not listen. And as for your mother – "

The old woman paused and then she suddenly took hold of Elissa's hand, something she had not done before.

"What do I do wrong?" she asked. "Tell me – am I too indulgent? Should I keep a tighter rein on him? Should I have kept your mother always with me and not let her roam free about the hillsides, as she always loved to do?"

Elissa's heart turned over at the thought of Mama years before escaping to the fresh air and the open moors, just as she herself loved to do now.

Maybe this was why she felt so happy in the garden as she must be stepping in her mother's own footsteps.

Lady Hartwell's hand was gripping hers tightly as if she was waiting for an answer.

"I don't think you could keep my cousin at home, if he did not want to be here," Elissa commented.

Lady Hartwell face twisted into a smile.

"No, indeed. I have often thought the very same thing. Of course I could not make him stay, but I do try to make him happy when he comes here."

Now the smile began to tremble and Elissa realised that her grandmother was on the verge of tears.

"Perhaps it is nothing to do with me at all, but some wildness, some wilfulness in the family that makes them want to behave so badly. Even you, Elissa, I have seen you wandering about in the garden looking out over the wall as if you should like to fly away."

"Oh, I am just taking Nelson out for a little air and the moors are very beautiful. I have never seen anything quite like them, living in London all my life."

It was a shock to Elissa to hear that Lady Hartwell had been watching her when she walked in the garden.

Would her grandmother decide to forbid her to go out? She could not bear it if she had to remain inside from now on.

But Lady Hartwell had become calmer.

"You do have a gentle touch, Elissa. My head still aches, but the pain is much easier. I think perhaps I may take a little nap."

"Lavender water is very soothing," Elissa told her.

"Indeed."

Lady Hartwell's eyes were closing.

"Thank you, my dear."

Elissa knelt beside the sofa until she could tell from her grandmother's regular breathing that she had fallen asleep.

Had she really just heard Lady Hartwell say,

'*Thank you*'?

'I have never heard her say 'thank you' to anybody before,' whispered Elissa. "Did you hear it, too, Nelson?" she asked the little pug, who crept out from under the sofa and licked her hand.

He whined and wagged his little curl of a tail at her, as if to say,

"Never mind all that – isn't it time for our walk?"

"Yes, yes, all right! We will go. Your Mistress is fast asleep and she won't be watching us from the window today. Perhaps we might even venture a little bit outside the garden – "

As she stepped out onto the terrace that ran around the house, Elissa caught her breath from the cold.

There were patches of whiteness here and there in the garden and for a moment she thought perhaps snow had fallen as the temperature was certainly low enough.

But when she went closer she saw that clumps of small white flowers were nodding their heads, braving the biting winds.

"Look there, Nelson!" cried Elissa. "Snowdrops! We had them in our garden in St. John's Wood. My Mama planted them, perhaps because she loved these – the ones that blossomed where she grew up, but I have never seen quite so many before!"

The sight filled her with joy and she ran through the garden with the little dog trotting behind, past all the neat flowerbeds and clipped bushes and up to the high wall and the gate that led to the outside world.

The top of the gate had a square cut out of it, which was criss-crossed with iron bars and Elissa peered through it and saw the enticing path stretching away over the hill.

"Come on, Nelson!" she called joyfully.

She lifted the latch and stepped through the gate.

The wind seemed stronger outside and it stung her cheeks and tugged at her skirts.

'*I feel as if I could fly*!' she mused, remembering Lady Hartwell's words and she spread out her arms and ran swiftly up the hill, following the path as it led away from The Towers.

65

She thought she would quickly be at the top of the hill, but the path was deceptive, for as soon as she came to what she thought was the top, yet another stretch of wild moorland revealed itself leading up towards the sky.

Soon Elissa had to stop and catch her breath as her lungs were aching with the cold air.

In the stormy sky she then noticed a dove, its wings pristine white against the grey clouds.

Buffeted and tossed by the strong wind, it battled on flying above the path.

Suddenly a swift shadow passed over Elissa's head and Nelson gave a little yelp of fear.

A dark bird of prey, its wings sharp as arrows, was hurtling towards the dove. At the last moment the white bird dodged away, turning back on itself and the predator shot past, rising high in the air as the wind caught it.

"Oh, quick, quick, be careful!" Elissa cried out, her heart in her mouth, as she watched the little dove fluttering down the hillside towards the shelter of some distant trees.

Then she looked up and saw high above her head, the falcon hanging with motionless wings, looking down at her and Nelson with its fierce far-seeing eyes.

"Your luck was out today!" she shouted up to it, as the dove had by now reached the safety of the trees.

The dark bird gave a shrill scream and with a flick of its sharp wings was gone.

Elissa could not help but admire its speed and skill in the air, but something about the bird's careless wildness reminded her of her cousin.

'And he is called Falcon, too – ' she whispered to herself, 'he comes and goes, just as he pleases, just like that wild bird of prey and I don't suppose that he cares too much who he hurts along the way."

It was too cold to climb any further.

She should turn back and leave her adventuring for another day when the sun was shining and the wind not so strong.

As she hurried back down the path, she wondered if her cousin would return from York that night.

She could not help but feel a bit uncomfortable and a little afraid at the thought of another evening spent with his dark mocking eyes upon her.

But the snowdrops would be gone from the garden, and the sun would then be shining warmly on a multitude of golden daffodils when Lord Hartwell deigned to return to Fellbrook Towers.

*

How strange it was to be in London again, Richard reflected, as he crossed Bond Street, dodging the hansom cabs and carriages that were rushing past with a clatter of hooves and a rattle of wheels.

After so many quiet days on the deserted Sussex Downs with just birdsong and the whisper of the wind for company, he had almost forgotten what it was like to be surrounded by people and vehicles.

Richard adjusted the heavy portfolio of paintings he was carrying into a comfortable position under his arm.

Which of the various smart galleries that lined the pavements should he approach?

It was a difficult decision.

Since he was only just starting out to be a painter, perhaps he should go to one of the smaller places, which had just a few pictures hanging on their walls.

But what was wrong with starting right at the top?

What if he was to boldly take his work into one of the larger establishments where the wide front windows gleamed in the sunshine, displaying row upon row of fine masterpieces?

Then Richard's heart began to quicken as he saw a familiar name over the door of a medium-sized gallery.

Gabriel Harker – the dealer who had bought all the paintings from his old home in Lanchberry Close!

As he stepped inside, the owner came towards him.

"I am afraid I am not taking on any new artists at present," he said in a cold haughty voice, eyeing Richard's portfolio.

But Richard did not hear him, for he was looking at one of the paintings hanging on the wall, of the cherry tree in blossom with the pretty girl standing beneath it, that he had once bought for his father.

Elissa, with her cloud of golden hair and her slim graceful figure –

"Sir, I must regret that if you are here looking for representation, I cannot help you," Mr. Harker was saying very close to Richard's ear.

Richard tore his eyes away from Elissa.

He looked down and noticed that his boots placed firmly on an expensive Oriental rug still had some Sussex mud on them.

Obviously Mr. Harker did not recognise him as the young gentleman he had bought the paintings from not so long ago.

In fact he now had his hand on Richard's arm and was about to forcibly eject him from the gallery.

"Mr. Harker, forgive me," said Richard, removing his felt hat, which was perfect for keeping his head warm while he was painting, but rather incorrect for Bond Street. "I should have introduced myself, Richard Stanfield!"

Mr. Harker dropped his hand from Richard's arm and gazed at him in astonishment.

"Mr. Stanfield, I am so sorry. I had no idea."

"Why should you? I have completely transformed myself and I am sure I must look completely disreputable."

He politely stepped off the beautiful rug.

"My mistake, Mr. Stanfield, I have been regrettably rude."

Mr. Harker was now looking at Richard's portfolio with interest.

"Have you brought any further paintings to sell?"

"Yes, in a manner of speaking – "

Much to his annoyance, he found himself blushing.

"These are – *my own work.*"

Mr. Harker now seemed at a loss for words and was staring at him with his mouth open, so Richard laid the portfolio down on a table and opened it up.

It was unbearable to watch him slowly turning over his paintings, holding them up the light, putting them down again.

"What do you think?" Richard managed to blurt out after a few painful moments.

Mr. Harker shook his head.

"You put me in a difficult position, Mr. Stanfield."

"You mean – they're no good?"

Richard felt a chill of despair run through him.

"Not exactly. Perhaps it would help if you could tell me what you are trying to achieve."

Richard looked up at the painting of the cherry tree, at the sunlight sparkling on its leaves, at the girl's glowing hair, a moment of beauty and happiness caught perfectly on the canvas.

"I'm trying to do what Leo Valentine does – did, I mean. The way that he catches things just as they are, only they seem even more real, more beautiful."

Mr. Harker sighed.

"A lifetime's work, Mr. Stanfield, to achieve such mastery."

"I'm determined to do it, whatever it takes."

"Well, this one shows promise."

Mr. Harker then picked up the picture Richard had called 'Old Newman' after the shepherd whose tiny figure appeared at the foot of the Downs.

Richard's mood now swung from utter misery to soaring hope, as he heard these words.

Mr. Harker propped the painting up onto the table and stepped back to look at it from a distance.

"The composition is unusual – stark and strong."

He turned back to the portfolio and closed it.

"These others are clearly the work of a painter still learning his craft. But Mr. Stanfield, I should be happy to take this one, 'Old Newman', and try to sell it for you."

"Oh, thank you," stammered Richard, feeling sad to think that the painting would no longer be his, but happy that Mr. Harker had agreed to take it.

"It isn't every day that a gentleman turns up to try and sell me his own work!" Mr. Harker said, going to the back of the shop and pouring two glasses of whisky.

"Whatever made you decide to embark on such a course?"

Richard explained about the sale of the house and the decision he had made to start a new life.

"I admire Leo Valentine so much," he said, looking at the cherry tree painting. "I should like to paint as well as he did one day."

Mr. Harker raised his glass.

"I salute your bravery," he told Richard, "you have been in Sussex I take it from the landscapes? Well – Mr. Stanfield, I advise you to take yourself somewhere where the countryside is much wilder, more dramatic. I shall be interested to see the results."

They raised their glasses in the sunlight that poured in brightly from the street and drank a toast to Richard's future endeavours.

*

"My dog has become a different creature," Lady Hartwell said, several weeks later, as faint March sunshine shone in through the parlour windows. "Before you came he was constantly barking and misbehaving."

Nelson rolled his black eyes up to look at her from where he lay peacefully in front of the fire and gave a little twitch of his curly tail.

"What have you been doing to him, Elissa? Have you been rubbing him with one of your herbal potions?"

"No! Although perhaps he might well enjoy some lavender water in his bath next time!"

"Well, I should not recognise him, he is as quiet as a lamb. And his waistline is much improved too as he was quite portly before."

Elissa knew that Nelson's calm behaviour and new, slim figure were entirely due to the long walks the two of them had been on while Lady Hartwell took her afternoon nap.

But she did not say so, as she still had a lingering fear her grandmother might easily forbid her to spend so much time out of doors.

"What do you think of my new gown, Elissa? Is it too garish? I don't want my grandson to think I am mutton dressed as lamb!"

Lady Hartwell took a slow turn about the room, her mauve silk skirts rustling across the carpet.

"It is perfect," enthused Elissa. "A soft colour, like the spring crocuses and the violets that are coming out just now in the garden. I think Lord Hartwell will approve."

Lady Hartwell gave a wry little smile.

"Ah, what do gentlemen ever know about fashion? Especially where their grandmothers are concerned, but I do like to look my best for him."

"Will he arrive in time for dinner?" asked Elissa, a little tremor of nervousness shaking her body.

"He says so, my dear, in his letter. But, of course, we can never be sure."

Lady Hartwell then sank down onto a sofa, her silk skirts settling around her like the petals of a flower.

"I do rather like this gown after all. Please send for Ernestine, so that it may be hung up ready for tonight. I must not crease it while I take my siesta."

"Of course and do you need anything else?"

Lady Hartwell gave Elissa a sideways look.

"Ah – I know what you are after. Well – go! Take yourself off to the garden. I must rest before tonight. Go!"

And the old lady turned away, a faint flush on her wrinkled cheeks, as she was already anticipating the arrival of her grandson.

The sun felt warmer today and so for the first time Elissa ventured out without her coat.

As she walked through the garden, making her way to the gate in the garden wall, the sweet scents of narcissi and wallflowers drifted through the air.

There were no flowers growing on the hillside, but its colour was subtly changing, turning a softer green in the distance.

It was not a day for hurrying and so Elissa strolled along her favourite path, enjoying the feel of the warm sun on her face until she found a little dip in the moor, where she sat down to rest for a while, Nelson at her side.

'Perhaps Lord Hartwell will leave me alone on this visit,' she said to herself, recalling her cousin's mocking dark eyes and teasing manner. 'If I stay quiet, he will not notice me next to Grandmama in her new gown.'

She felt her anxiety melting away in the warmth of the sun and within a few moments her eyes closed and she began to doze.

But it was not a peaceful sleep she fell into.

Immediately Elissa found herself in a vivid dream. She was still sitting on the hill, but the grass and heather had turned from a soft greeny-brown to a bright gold that almost hurt her eyes.

She was not alone.

Someone was kneeling behind her and soft hands as gentle as the warm sunshine were stroking her hair.

"Mama?" she exclaimed and tried to get up, but her limbs were heavy and would not move.

Something small and white was drifting down out of the blue sky, twirling round and round until it fell into Elissa's lap.

It was a small white feather and as she looked at it, she remembered the dove she had seen a few weeks before, escaping the talons of the falcon.

"What is it, Mama?" she asked, fighting against the heaviness in her body. "What does it mean?"

And then the brilliant gold hillside melted away and her eyes flew open as she woke up, startled by the sound of her own voice.

Nelson was there gazing at her and making a little whining noise.

"It's all right, Poppet," she told him. "Just a dream, that's all. Come, let's go back."

Suddenly she no longer felt safe alone on the empty hillside.

*

"I'm making a go of it!" trumpeted Richard, raising his champagne glass, as he sat with Monty in one of their old haunts in Piccadilly. "One of my paintings is now in a Bond Street gallery!"

"Steady on, man!" replied Monty, looking doubtful. "How much whisky did you say you've had? It's not sold yet, is it? Your painting? You've not actually the cash in your hand yet, have you?"

"Oh, Monty, stop talking like a lawyer!" Richard retorted, trying to quell the excitement welling up inside him. "Mr. Harker thinks my landscapes show promise."

"I cannot see the attraction of that subject myself. Why don't you try your hand at portraits? Beautiful girls, that's what you should be painting – "

Richard shuddered visibly, recalling his sketches of Mercedes with her gleaming dark eyes and her mane of red hair he had burned before he left London.

"So, anyway, old friend – what's next?" Monty was asking.

Richard then explained that he intended to take Mr. Harker's advice and go to more remote areas with dramatic scenery.

"You know, somewhere in the North of the country – Yorkshire, perhaps."

Monty looked disappointed.

"Too far away, old man, we'll never get to see you. Stay in London!"

"I just can't afford it. Where would I live? And I'd never be able to keep up with you, Monty, going out for dinner and champagne all the time."

"You could quite easily afford it, Richard, if you did what I have always advised and claimed your money back from that evil woman."

Richard shook his head.

"I don't know where she is and I don't want to."

"What was her name again?" Monty asked, dipping into his pocket to pull out a crumpled newspaper cutting.

"Leave it, please do!" Richard huffed.

But he could not help looking down at the snippet of paper that Monty was unfolding on the table as he read out slowly and deliberately,

"Lady Talbot's delightful salon was illuminated this weekend by the presence of a recent arrival from South America – the exquisite heiress Señorita Mercedes de Rosario. We are sure it will not be long before we see her name again – perhaps in the Engagements column, as she is guaranteed to turn the head of every young Society gentleman she meets."

"It's her, isn't it?" Monty insisted. "She's taken all your money, old man, and now reinvented herself as an heiress!"

Richard felt suddenly sick.

He sincerely wished he had not had quite so much champagne and whisky to drink.

The last thing in the world he wanted to do was to see Mercedes's beautiful deceitful face again.

He would leave London first thing tomorrow.

Yorkshire was a bleak and cold place – or so he had heard and, as he took up his brush to capture its forbidding hills and moors on canvas, he would soon forget all about the temptress who had caused him so much pain.

CHAPTER SIX

'Why did I worry so that my cousin might pay too much attention to me?' thought Elissa, as she sat down at table that evening in the dining room at Fellbrook Towers.

She watched closely as Lord Hartwell settled into the chair opposite her.

He seemed lost in another world, his handsome face as dark as a thundercloud.

Even Lady Hartwell's beautiful new mauve gown, which gleamed exquisitely in the soft candlelight, attracted no comment from him.

"Dearest," she began in a rather tentative voice, "I asked the butler to send up the very best champagne. Will you not try a little?"

Lord Hartwell roused himself and glared at the tiny bubbles drifting upwards in his glass.

"Such extravagance," he growled.

Lady Hartwell looked shocked.

"But Falcon, I thought – you are here so rarely – "

"In future," he scowled, "*I* shall choose which wine is brought to table."

"Of course, my dear, but the bottle has been opened for you, it will not keep."

He picked up his glass and drained it in one gulp and then grabbed his fork and moved the food around on his plate, but he did not eat any.

After a few moments, Lady Hartwell tried again to engage him in conversation,

"What news of the horse you went to try last time you were here? Did you buy it, my dear?"

Lord Hartwell nodded, his eyes on his plate.

"And how does it run?"

"It doesn't. Useless beast – they told me it was a perfect Pegasus and it would fly over every obstacle and beat all competition."

He shoved his plate away so that it skidded along the polished surface of the table and held up his glass for the butler to replenish.

"Yes!" he shouted, as the champagne flowed from the bottle. "A toast to Black Prince – the most calamitous beast that ever stepped onto a Racecourse. Fell at the first fence, broke its neck and darned near broke the bank as well!"

"Oh, poor creature!" Elissa piped up before she could stop herself.

Her cousin glared at her, his black brows creased in a frown.

"I doubt it felt a thing. Save your pity for the poor ruined owner it left behind!"

"Oh, Falcon! Surely you did not make some foolish bet on this horse," Lady Hartwell tried to admonish him.

"And what if I did? My fortune is mine to do with whatever I choose, what gentleman does not like to gamble a little? The horse was well-bred, it had good form. They told me it was a certain thing and I thought I would make back the vast sum I paid for it."

"Oh, Falcon – "

Lady Hartwell's voice was trembling.

Her grandson stood up, his face red with anger.

"I have no appetite! Especially for your nagging, Grandmama."

And then he strode out of the dining room.

Lady Hartwell sat still and dabbed at her eyes with her napkin.

"May I fetch you anything?" Elissa asked her.

"No, my dear. My peace of mind is shattered, there is nothing to help me. Oh, how do I wish these young men would not risk so much at the Racecourse!"

"Perhaps my cousin has learned his lesson."

Lady Hartwell sighed and shook her head.

"I fear not. The remedy is always to try again and place some other reckless bet to regain what has been lost. I have seen it so many times with other hot-headed young men. And when the money runs out – they will then wager anything – their land, even their fine houses that have been in their families for centuries."

"I am sure it will not come to that!" cried Elissa. "Your grandson would never – "

"The Towers belongs to Falcon," Lady Hartwell interrupted, "it came to him when his father died and I may live here if he so chooses, but it is his to throw away upon the Racecourse and nothing I say will stop him."

A chill of fear ran through Elissa's veins.

Lady Hartwell belonged at The Towers. She could not imagine the old lady making her home anywhere else.

But perhaps it might not go so far as this.

She remembered a favourite saying of her Mama's, whenever she had been worried that there would be no money to pay a bill.

Now, she told it to Lady Hartwell,

"Let us not meet trouble halfway."

The old lady looked at her, brows raised in surprise. "What?"

"I mean you must not worry too much as so often what we fear the most does not come about. Mama used to say so."

"Ah!"

Lady Hartwell's arched brows sank into a frown.

"I thought I had heard that phrase before. Some nonsense that Helena picked up from her nanny. Well – Elissa, I can tell you now that all my worst fears came true when your mother ran away. Why should I now expect that things will turn out for the best with Falcon?"

She then stood up and swept away from the table, her mauve skirts whispering over the floor.

It felt odd to be all alone in the dining room, just as she had been on her first night at Fellbrook Towers.

For politeness sake, Elissa tasted a little of each of the courses that the butler brought to her, and she was glad that she did, as despite his silence, she detected a look of pleasure in his faded grey eyes.

She even took a couple of sips of the champagne, and felt it run through her body like sparkling sunshine.

The feeling reminded her of her dream out on the hillside earlier that day.

She was certain that she had felt her Mama's hands touching her hair in the dream. But why had she seen the white feather drifting down to fall in her lap?

It had looked so beautiful, glinting like snow in the bright sunlight. She could still see it now if she closed her eyes against the glow of the candlelight.

What was the meaning of it?

In the other dream where Mama had come to her, she had been given a date written in a book, which turned out to be the date of her dear Papa's death.

But a feather from a little white dove?

What was she supposed to make of that?

The butler approached and asked if Miss Valentine would be taking coffee in the drawing room.

"Thank you, but no," she told him. "I think I shall retire early this evening."

She ran up the wide staircase and along the landing and into her cosy bedroom where, as he did every night, Marmalade lay on the sofa, purring while he watched Ellen warming Elissa's nightgown in front of the fire.

Ellen was bursting to hear all that had happened at dinner.

"Did he speak to you, miss?" she asked.

"Lord Hartwell? No, Ellen, he did not! I might not have been in the room for all the notice he took of me."

"Oh, miss!"

Ellen looked disappointed.

"But don't feel sorry for me."

Elissa sat on the sofa and took Marmalade onto her lap, stroking his fur and listening to his purring grow loud with ecstasy.

"When he was here before, his manner was teasing and unkind and I would much rather he left me alone."

"They say, miss, that 'e has – lost all 'is fortune," Ellen blurted out, looking sideways at Elissa.

"Now who told you that?" demanded Elissa. "You should not listen to the other servants' gossip."

"I could not 'elp it, miss. I went to fetch your 'ot water and his Lordship's manservant, who came with 'im from London, was in the pantry talking to Mrs. Nantwich."

Elissa could no longer resist asking what Ellen had overheard.

"Why, miss, the man said 'e be very afraid for 'is position if Lord Hartwell did not mend 'is ways. And then Mrs. Nantwich told 'im that we would all be out of a job if things went on as they 'ave been."

"That does sound very bad, but we do not know the truth of the matter. Only Lord Hartwell could tell us that and he is keeping his own counsel. So do not fret, Ellen. I am sure that all will be well."

She remembered her cousin's troubled face and the way that he had snapped at Lady Hartwell. But Elissa said nothing of what she had witnessed at dinner. She did not want to add to her maid's anxieties.

"I shall retire early tonight," she said. "Ellen, why don't you take Marmalade with you? It is very warm and comforting when he sleeps on one's feet."

"You are so kind, miss, but my bed is in Ernestine's room and I don't think she would approve, even if I could persuade 'im to leave you!"

Elissa laughed.

"Oh, dear, no! Ernestine would be horrified! She would imagine Marmalade's ginger hairs all over her smart black dress. That would never do!"

And she was rather relieved to see that Ellen, too, was looking amused at the idea of Lady Hartwell's fierce French maid coming face to face with Marmalade in her boudoir.

"Please, Ellen, don't think any more over what you overheard. I will speak to Lord Hartwell tomorrow and see if I can find out the truth."

As Elissa lay in bed, watching the fire sink down to dull red embers in the grate, she reflected at what a strange eventful day it had been.

And then Marmalade jumped up onto the bed and curled himself up on her feet.

She fell into a deep and peaceful sleep.

*

Next morning the world outside Fellbrook Towers was swathed in a thick white mist.

After breakfast Elissa stepped out into the garden, but after just a few moments her hair and her clothes were wet with the drops of moisture drifting through the air.

"We should not stay out too long, Nelson," she said to the little pug. "There is nothing to be seen and we will get wet and cold."

The mist hung all around like a thick white blanket and only the gravel and the nearest flowerbed were visible.

Upstairs in her parlour, Lady Hartwell was nervous and distracted, constantly picking up her embroidery and dropping it, as she rose from the sofa to pace up and down.

"What am I to do?" she fretted. "He will leave us again, I just know he will, and I still don't know the half of what has been going on. How much has he lost? He will not tell me.

"Oh, how I hate this fog, I can feel it creeping in through the window frames. Draw the curtains, Elissa! I cannot bear to look at it."

Elissa drew the curtains and lit several candles as by now the parlour was particularly gloomy.

"*What will he do?*" Lady Hartwell continued, "I am sure he is planning to leave us again and without speaking a word to me – "

"He cannot go anywhere this morning or he would get lost on the moor. I could hardly see my hand in front of my face when I went out just now."

"Go to him, Elissa! Tell him he must stay, at least until luncheon."

Elissa felt her face grow hot at the idea of trying to tell her impetuous cousin what he should do.

But Lady Hartwell insisted.

"I am out of favour, I know he will just send me away with an unkind word. But he will listen to you. Go and find him, Elissa!"

Her heart was beating faster as she approached the library door, where one of the footmen had directed her.

She tapped softly on it and heard her cousin's voice as he barked,

"Come!"

The book-lined library was filled with a grey fog of strong-smelling cigar smoke – almost as thick as the soft moorland mist outside.

Lord Hartwell was nowhere to be seen, but Elissa noticed a smoke-ring rising above the back of one of the leather armchairs by the fire and she walked towards it.

Her cousin was reading a newspaper and did not look up as she approached.

"*Trojan Warrior, Bold Buccaneer, Pots of Gold.* Which? I don't know, I don't know – " he muttered to himself.

Elissa stepped a little closer and at last he saw her.

"What, Governess?" he called. "Have you come to borrow a book to read? Help yourself."

He waved haughtily at the rows of leather-bound volumes that covered the walls of the library.

"No, I – " she stammered, struggling to keep from blushing.

"What, then?" he demanded impatiently, "I suppose Grandmama has sent you here to pester me with something or other."

He sighed and thrust the newspaper at her.

"Quick, Governess. Which would you choose from all these useless nags?"

Elissa glanced down the page quickly and realised that he had given her a list of horses in a race.

"I know nothing about racehorses," she blurted out.

"So? Nor, it seems do I, judging by my luck on the Racecourse. I have studied the form, I have watched the stupid creatures prancing around the paddock and yet still I cannot seem to pick a winner. So – Governess – you do it! *Go on!*"

He laughed, breathing a cloud of bitter cigar smoke into her face.

Elissa recoiled.

His rudeness made her skin shiver.

She felt tears spring into her eyes and the long list of horses' names faded into a blur as she tried to look at it.

The big brass clock on the library mantelpiece gave a little whirr and began striking.

It was eleven o'clock.

"Curses! Is it so late already?" Lord Hartwell gave an angry shout. "Get on with it, girl! The race is at two-thirty and the Racecourse is many miles away! Make your choice!"

She blinked to clear her vision.

Trojan Warrior. Bold Buccaneer. Flight of Fancy. Pots of Gold. Wings of a Dove. Egremont.

Suddenly she seemed to feel her Mama's hands on her hair again and saw the white feather drifting before her, circling down and brushing one of the printed names with its fine filaments as it fell on the page of the newspaper.

"*Wings of a Dove*," she whispered to him. "That is the one."

"What on earth do you mean? Are you out of your mind? *Wings of a Dove* is a rank outsider!"

Elissa was trembling as she persisted,

"*That* is the horse you must choose."

The bookshelves were shimmering like a mirage all around her, her head felt full of mist and cigar smoke and she did not know if she was awake or if she had fallen into another dream.

"Whoa, steady!" her cousin exclaimed and seized her arm roughly.

"Don't get a fit of the vapours on me!"

He pushed her down on one of the leather chairs.

Elissa dropped her head into her hands and as she struggled to clear her mind, she heard a sharp rap at the library door.

"My Lord, if you are still set to go we must leave – there is mist and mizzle over the moor and our pace must be slow."

Elissa recognised the gruff voice of Oldroyd, the coachman, who had brought her to The Towers.

Lord Hartwell began cursing angrily.

"I am held back at every turn. Impeded, hampered by fools!"

"We will lose our way, my Lord, if we go too fast," the coachman told him patiently but Lord Hartwell was not listening.

"My charming little cousin here – the Governess – look! She has picked out what will no doubt be the slowest horse in the race! *Wings of a Dove*! What do you make of that, Oldroyd?"

He flapped the newspaper in front of his face.

The stout man screwed up his eyes to read the page.

"The odds are very good, my Lord. Your winnings will be 'igh, if the mare wins."

"But the creature has never won a race!"

Oldroyd was still peering at the page.

"Well, my Lord, I cannot advise you. But this one is bred to stay and to jump. And an 'orse of that ilk can be slow to come to its prime."

Suddenly the library seemed to be full of the same golden light that had shone over the hill in Elissa's dream.

The mist was breaking up and long bars of sunshine were shining in through the window.

"So it is then," Lord Hartwell trumpeted, throwing his cigar into the fire. "*Everything* on *Wings of a Dove*. Let's go, Oldroyd. And woe betide you, Governess, if it loses."

'What have I done?' Elissa thought, as the two men left the library, their boots thudding over the wooden floor.

But deep inside she knew that she could not have made any other choice.

She had seen the feather from her dream again – the dove's feather – and it had fallen exactly where the rank outsider's name was printed – *Wings of a Dove*.

All she could do now was wait and pray that all would be well.

*

Richard's legs ached as he climbed up the rocky path, peering through clouds of mist drifting towards him.

'I just need to get a little higher and I'm sure I will find the sunshine,' he told himself. 'What a strange wild place this is.'

It seemed even wilder because he could not actually see where he was going.

He was climbing stoutly and he was pretty sure that there would be a steep drop on the other side of the path, but beyond it was all mysterious and quite unlike anywhere he had ever been before.

He had spent the night in an attic room in a tiny cottage listening to owls crying and the rustle of the wind under the roof slates.

And Mrs. Oldroyd, his grey-haired landlady, had served him a bowl of thick porridge for his breakfast, and listened in total silence as he had explained to her that he was an artist and that he was delighted to be visiting the wonderful County of Yorkshire.

He was feeling quite unsettled by the time he had finished the porridge and the silent Mrs. Oldroyd then put a large packet wrapped in greaseproof paper in front of him.

"Ah, sandwiches! Just the ticket. Thank you very much, Mrs. Oldroyd!" he had smiled at his landlady.

She nodded and disappeared into her kitchen – and Richard had stepped out into this eerie white world that seemed to muffle all the sounds around him and coated his clothes with droplets of water.

'Onwards and upwards, Richard,' he told himself, forcing his tired legs to keep going.

He was now recalling Monty's words just before he left London,

"A Yorkshireman will never use two words when one will do!" he had advised.

Richard had not taken much notice at the time, but it might explain why Mrs. Oldroyd scarcely seemed to use any words at all.

Now the mist was thinning and up ahead of him, he heard a bird singing – a skylark.

He quickened his pace until he found his head and then his whole body emerging from the mist as he reached the top of the hill.

If he had been more musical, he might have burst into song as he there stood looking down on the great lake of mist spread out for miles across the countryside below him, and shining white under the golden light of the sun.

It was one of the most glorious sights he had ever seen.

'If I was a genius like Turner,' he mused, 'I might be able to capture it in paint, but I have a long way to go yet before I'm as good as him!'

And feeling hungry after such a long climb, he sat down and opened the packet of sandwiches.

They were made with thick coarse bread and when he opened one of them up to see what was inside, he burst out laughing.

'Well, this is a far cry from Mayfair!' he smiled as he took his first hearty bite of Mrs. Oldroyd's bread-and-dripping.

It did not taste too bad at all and as he munched away, something very remarkable started to happen.

The mist in front of him began to melt away under the sun's rays and the top of a ruined stone arch surrounded by broken and crumbling walls emerged.

He caught his breath as he realised this beautiful ruin must have been just below him hidden in the mist all the time he had been climbing up the path.

He sat very still, hugging his knees, as he waited for the last clouds of vapour to disappear and for the whole of the mysterious building to reveal itself to him.

*

"I am certain my cousin will be back soon," said Elissa, thinking that at any moment she must send for some lavender water to calm her grandmother's nerves.

She felt much in need of some for herself, as all day long her heart had been fluttering with fear every time she thought of what had happened in the library, and now her head was aching with a sharp intense pain.

"But you do know what he is like!" Lady Hartwell moaned, her voice grown thin with constant complaining. "What if he runs off again, and leaves us none-the-wiser as to what he is up to, while he gambles away all the estate?"

Elissa could not reply to this.

With all her heart and soul she hoped she would never see Lord Hartwell again.

Let him never never come back to The Towers!

All through luncheon and the long bright afternoon she had kept to herself what she had done.

She could not confess to her grandmother that she had picked out the name of a horse in a race and given it to her cousin.

How could she possibly explain her dream and the strange feeling that had come over her in the library?

When *Wings of the Dove* lost the race, which surely it would, then she, Elissa, would be responsible for the loss of Fellbrook Towers and the ruin of the Hartwell family.

Her heart heavy with despair, Elissa turned to gaze out of the window at her beloved hilltop and the path that stretched away over the moor.

Far away in the distance two riders, one on a black horse were approaching at a breakneck pace.

'They look so like men who fear nothing, who have nothing left to lose,' Elissa thought and felt sick with fear.

"Please excuse me, Lady Hartwell. I am feeling a little unwell."

At all costs she had to tear herself away from the parlour and find somewhere quiet and then decide what she must do, as she could only believe that the worst must have happened.

CHAPTER SEVEN

As Richard bounded back down the steep path, his rucksack filled with many sketches of the beautiful ruined building that had risen out of the mist, his main worry now was how he was going to pass another meal in the taciturn company of Mrs. Oldroyd.

'How can I get her to speak to me?' he wondered. 'I could ask if there is a Mr. Oldroyd and then she might talk to me about him – but what if there isn't? If she is a widow, she'll be upset and then it could be days before she says another word to me!'

When he arrived at the tiny cottage, the kitchen was filled with the delicious aroma of boiled ham, whilst Mrs. Oldroyd was busy stirring something on the stove.

"That smells quite marvellous!" enthused Richard.

Mrs. Oldroyd nodded to him, just as she had done when he left that morning and carried on stirring.

"Oh, by the way," he continued, braving her stern expression, "what is that ruin in the valley with the arches and broken walls. It looks like it was once some kind of Church?"

"The Old Priory," Mrs. Oldroyd told him curtly in her thick Yorkshire accent.

"Ah! *The Old Priory*!" Richard repeated, after he had worked out what she was saying. "I thought it must be something like that."

He was just tucking into a plateful of fragrant ham

with boiled potatoes and thick parsley sauce when a stout man pushed open the cottage door.

"How do!" he greeted Richard in a gruff voice.

Then he turned to Mrs. Oldroyd.

"This be the lodger, lass?"

Anyone less like a lass than Mrs. Oldroyd with her grey hair and dour expression, Richard could not imagine.

But she nodded in reply to the question.

"Well, you can send 'im away, if you want!"

The man reached inside his coat and pulled out a fat envelope, which he slapped down on the table.

Mrs. Oldroyd's eyes widened and she clasped the cooking spoon to her apron front.

"Yes, lass," the man continued, "'is Lordship, God save 'im, 'as come good at last. He's won back all 'e lost and more and I've made a tidy bit meself too. We shan't end up without a penny to our names. We're saved!"

Richard was so intrigued that hungry as he was, he stopped eating to listen.

Mrs. Oldroyd's face frowned.

"Until the next time," she murmured. "I'll place no trust in yon feckless lad."

She put down another plate on the table and ladled some food onto it.

Richard stood up and extended a hand.

"Richard Stanfield – Mr. Oldroyd, I presume?"

"Aye, that be right. Lord Hartwell's coachman at Fellbrook Towers."

He sat down and started eating.

Richard was longing to hear more about what had happened, but Mr. Oldroyd had fallen into the same silence that afflicted his wife.

After a few moments, observing that Mr. Oldroyd's dinner was almost eaten, Richard suggested tentatively,

"Perhaps I should go and find some other lodgings now that your situation has changed?"

Mrs. Oldroyd picked up the envelope and pulled out the five pound notes that had been stuffed inside.

She counted them out and put them into her pocket. It looked like a great deal more money than she would ever make from Richard's modest payments, even if he stayed for months.

But she turned to him and shook her head.

"No, lad! Stay. 'ard times may come again with a man like 'is Lordship at the 'elm. And you'll not be under my feet if you're out all day at your paintin'."

"If the Missus says stay on, I'm certain you're right welcome," Mr. Oldroyd added, pushing his plate away.

"Although if that young woman keeps on pickin' winners, we'll 'ave no need of a lodger."

"Really? Who do you mean?" Richard asked him, hoping he would continue talking.

"She be a real angel in disguise and it's no mistake. Told his Lordship to back the outsider for us and the mare came in at 100 to 1!"

Mrs. Oldroyd clattered the plates together loudly as she cleared the table.

"Pure chance, Arthur, and nothin' else!"

"No, lass!"

Mr. Oldroyd's broad face turned a little red.

"The girl 'as a gift. She turned white as a sheet and looked as if she'd faint away as she told us the winner."

"But who is she?" Richard asked, fascinated by the story.

"Lord Hartwell's cousin, fresh up from London and never been on a Racecourse in 'er life!"

Richard smiled away to himself, imagining a pale, haughty Society girl, performing a fit of the vapours as she attempted to guess which horse might restore her cousin's fortunes.

Surely Mrs. Oldroyd was correct – it could only be pure chance that had made this girl guess the winner.

Richard was glad that he was going to stay on at the cottage as he was looking forward to the next instalment of gossip from Fellbrook Towers and it sounded like a hotbed of scandal and intrigue.

And Mr. Oldroyd, who was now explaining that he lived most of the time in a room over the coach house, so that he was always to hand should his Lordship need him, would be in a good position to provide it.

*

Elissa lay curled up under the warm bedcovers with Marmalade in her arms.

Several times through the long afternoon she had thought of running away from The Towers and heading off along the secret green path that led over the hill.

But her cousin had returned and she pictured him coming after her on his swift black horse, and knew that she would be completely at his mercy as he swooped down upon her just like the deadly bird of prey, *his namesake*.

"Miss!"

Ellen was shaking her shoulder.

"Lady Hartwell is askin' for you!"

Elissa rolled over in the bed, a sick feeling of dread in her stomach. Surely by now her grandmother must know what she had done?

"I cannot go, Ellen, I am not well!" she whimpered.

"But miss!"

"I cannot, Ellen, I cannot!"

Elissa pulled the covers over her head and after a moment heard the door click shut as Ellen left the room.

From down below she could hear voices shouting and doors banging and to shut the sound out, she buried her face in Marmalade's soft fur and let his rumbling purr fill her ears.

Suddenly he slid out of her arms and jumped to the floor, growling and fluffing his tail like a feather duster.

"What is it?" she asked him, sitting up and pulling the covers around her.

The shouting now seemed to be coming from the landing outside her room.

"*Where is she?* Come on out and show yourself!"

It was her cousin's voice and now he was banging on the door.

'No!' Elissa determined, her heart racing, and she wished that she had thought to turn the key in the lock after Ellen had left.

But it was too late.

The handle was now turning and then he was there in her bedroom, mud on his riding boots and his black hair still tousled from his wild gallop across the moors.

"Well, you shy violet! What do you have to say for yourself?" he shouted.

Elissa could not bear to look at him and instead she watched Marmalade, who was backing away, hissing and spitting, his back arched in a hoop.

"What can you be doing hiding away in here?" he demanded.

And then to Elissa's horror, her cousin seized the

edge of her satin quilt and pulled it off the bed, leaving her stranded before him, clad in just her petticoat.

Now he took hold of her hands in a grip so tight that she winced with pain and pulled her onto her feet.

"I'm so so sorry," she gasped. "Please let me go!"

"Out of the question!" he cried and, to her utmost astonishment, she saw that he was smiling at her. "I shall *never*, never let you go after today!"

And he tugged at her hands and spun her round as if she was a little child.

"No, stop! Please!" she called and suddenly found herself caught in his arms, pressed tightly against his velvet riding coat.

"My angel, Elissa," he screamed and she caught the vapours of whisky and wine on this breath.

"What – ?

"*Wings of a Dove*! Came in first at 100 to 1!" he howled. "*We did it*!"

Shocked to her very core, Elissa gazed into his dark eyes.

"Oh, yes, my little angel! We did it!"

He bent towards her, as if he was going to kiss her lips.

"No, no – please – let me go!" she pleaded and felt his rough cheek graze her face as she turned away.

Now he was touching her hair, pulling out the pins and running his fingers through it so that it fell in a cloud over her shoulders.

"You even look like an angel," he muttered. "So sweet and innocent in your petticoat with your beautiful golden hair, which, I do confess, I have wanted to see loose and free like this since the first moment I met you."

She struggled to get away, beating her fists against his arms and after a moment he let her go.

"Please forgive me, cousin," he declared. "I should be kneeling at your feet, thanking you from the depths of my heart for what you have done."

"I – did nothing!"

He then threw back his head and laughed, swaying a little on his feet, as if he was drunk.

"Nothing? A brilliant '*nothing*' that has restored to me everything I had lost!"

He frowned suddenly.

"I stood to lose so much more – almost everything – if *Wings of a Dove* had not flown very sweetly past the winning post. I had so little money left that a good part of the estate was up for wager!"

"I did not know that," mumbled Elissa. "I just don't know why I picked *Wings of a Dove*! I am glad it won, but it was just a lucky chance – "

Her cousin made as if to sweep an imaginary hat from his head and made a low mocking bow to her.

"Never say that, my angel, as I won't believe you. And now, I must take my leave – for you are clearly not used to entertaining gentlemen in your boudoir – and since you have brought me such amazing luck, your wish must be my command!"

And as good as his word, he swaggered out, leaving Elissa so weak with shock that she collapsed onto the sofa.

"Miss? Are you feelin' better?"

It was Ellen, who had crept into the room carrying a mountain of packages piled in her arms.

"Ellen – what are these?" asked Elissa, reaching to catch the topmost parcel, as it slipped from her arms.

"His Lordship, miss, brought them today."

"But – "

Through a tear in the brown paper, Elissa could see the gleam of a pale-coloured silken fabric.

"If all these are gifts from Lord Hartwell, I cannot accept them."

Ellen's face fell.

"Miss, 'er Ladyship told me to bring them to you. You must open them, she said, as you will need the things for tonight."

Elissa's heart contracted with a tight cold pain.

It did not feel right that her cousin should be giving all these presents to her and yet if her grandmother insisted, she would have to accept them.

"Look, miss!"

Ellen put the packages down and began to tear the brown paper from the parcel on Elissa's lap. Inside was an exquisite gown of grey silk, trimmed with a delicate rose-pink collar and cuffs.

"And miss! There is this!"

Ellen was holding up a shawl, as soft in colour as mother-of-pearl.

"And these!"

The maid then unwrapped a cluster of pink ribbons, threaded through with gleaming pearls.

When Elissa stayed silent, sitting on the sofa, Ellen carried the clothes to the bed, and laid them out ready for her to wear.

"Come on, miss – or you'll be late for dinner!" she urged.

The fine silk of the dress felt so chill and smooth as she slid her arms into the sleeves and she definitely missed the familiar warmth of her old black dress.

'I am sorry, Papa, to lay aside my mourning clothes so soon,' she whispered, 'but grey too is sometimes worn for mourning. I hope you will forgive me.'

Lord Hartwell raised his glass and beamed at Elissa across the laden dinner able.

"Well, Governess, do you like your new dress?"

His eyes were bloodshot and his hand shook a little, and a drop of foaming champagne spilled onto the damask tablecloth.

"It becomes her well," Lady Hartwell chipped in.

Her eyes were very bright and she looked dazed, as if she did not quite understand the wonderful change in her grandson's fortunes.

"From the finest dressmaker in York," he was now saying. "I'd so rather see you all in pink like a lovely rosy angel, but I know your modest tastes, cousin, so I chose the grey."

Elissa's skin shivered as she felt his eyes running over her. The silk felt so thin and light compared with the wool of the black dress she normally wore.

Lord Hartwell drained his glass.

"And tomorrow – sweet angel – we shall look over *The Racing Times* again – "

This was what Elissa had been really dreading.

Had he not heard what she had said to him when he came into her bedroom?

Lady Hartwell was still looking confused.

"Dearest, you have been extremely fortunate today. Surely you cannot expect Elissa to repeat the lucky guess she made this morning? Anyway racing and everything to do with it is a gentleman's pastime and not something that a young lady should concern herself with."

Her grandson sighed impatiently.

"Darling Grandmama! My excellent fortune today is entirely my sweet little cousin's doing. Have I not told you a hundred times already? By some wonderful, magical intuition s*he chose the winning horse for me!*"

Lady Hartwell turned to Elissa.

"Yes, Falcon, so you keep telling me. But, Elissa, you know nothing about horses or Racecourses, do you?"

"No, Lady Hartwell. I don't know what happened. I had a strange dream, and then I picked out *Wings of a Dove* – and I was so frightened, and I was sure I had made the wrong choice."

"You see, Falcon! It's all nonsense, Elissa does not know what she is doing. You have had a very lucky win. Just be grateful and let us have no more of these infernal wagers."

Lord Hartwell gave her a dark look.

"Grandmama, don't push the point any further," he grunted in a low voice, "or I may find myself asking you to mind your own business!"

Then he turned to Elissa, a smile hovering on his lips.

"Now, angel, if you have eaten and drunk your fill, I think it could be time for you to retire and may I wish you many sweet and very lucky dreams – all of which you must remember for tomorrow morning, when you come to the library."

As he winked at her, he downed yet another glass of champagne.

*

"I cannot do it!" cried Elissa, her voice catching in her throat with fear. "Please, don't ask me!"

Her legs were trembling and she feared that at any moment they might give way beneath her and she would tumble down onto the purple rug that stood in front of the library fireplace.

Her cousin scowled at her and his face was drawn and sallow in the morning sun that streamed in through the library windows.

"It is a simple request, is it not?" he leered. "Here is a list of runners in the three o'clock race this afternoon. All I ask is that you choose *one*."

He thrust *The Racing Times* into her face.

The printed list of names swam in front of her eyes and she could not make them out as she was close to tears.

"What in the name of Heaven is wrong with you!" he shouted suddenly. "What foolish games are you playing with me?"

Elissa swallowed, trying to clear her voice.

"I am not playing – any games," she quavered.

"I don't believe you, you ungrateful little witch," he hissed. "Look at you in that fine blue gown, just one of the many lovely dresses I sent to your room yesterday. What are you thinking of by refusing so simple a request!"

"I did not ask you for anything," she stuttered. "I – did not think the horse I chose would win – I don't know how I did it."

Lord Hartwell came up to her and took her elbows in a painful grip.

"You told Grandmama you dreamed of the winner, surely that must be how you did it! Well – what were your dreams last night?"

Elissa shook her head.

She did not like to tell her cousin that she had not slept at all after all he had said to her over dinner.

She had stayed awake and terrified all through the

long dark hours, dreading that he would ask her to pick yet another winner.

Lord Hartwell swore and let go of her arms.

He paced up and down in front of the fire, hitting the palm of one hand with the fist of the other, glaring at Elissa as if he would have preferred to be striking her.

"I can easily pay off all my debts with what I won yesterday," he said in a slow measured tone, as if he was explaining it to a small child.

"*But it is just not enough.* If I am to live as a true gentleman should do, then I must substantially increase my fortune. And you, Elissa, are deliberately preventing me from doing that, you insolent little witch!"

It was only last night, Elissa reflected, that he had been calling her an angel.

"Don't just stand there, staring at me!" he roared suddenly and then he was running at her, hurling one of the chairs that stood between them out of his way.

Elissa tried to dodge away from him, but the heel of her boot caught in the rug and she fell heavily, catching her shoulder against a small table in front of the fire.

"How do!"

A deep voice then cried out in a strong Yorkshire accent.

"The lady is down!"

It was Oldroyd, dressed for the road in his caped coat and heavy boots.

"I am all right," Elissa gasped, struggling to stand up, although a stabbing pain ran from her shoulder all the way down her arm.

"Really, I am absolutely fine."

Lord Hartwell was hovering over her his brows knit

together in an angry frown and she could not bear the mere thought of him touching her.

"Twas a heavy fall, miss," muttered Oldroyd.

"Well – she is on her feet, she cannot have come to much harm," Lord Hartwell snarled. "I suppose it's time to leave for the Racecourse? I warn you, Oldroyd, I have no hot tips for today, thanks to this stubborn creature."

"Ah!" the coachman replied and Elissa thought that his wide red face held a kindly expression.

"We cannot expect to be lucky every day!"

"I do expect it, Oldroyd. I do. And I don't like to be contradicted and disobeyed by those who could easily help me if they wished to do so."

Lord Hartwell kicked at the leg of the sofa, leaving a dent in the polished wood.

Oldroyd then took a step towards him watching him closely, as if he was an unruly horse.

"Perhaps the young lady has worn 'erself out with 'er efforts yesterday. We can wager small amounts today, as I'm sure she'll come up trumps again another time."

"She had better!" smirked Lord Hartwell.

And without another word to Elissa, he stamped out of the library.

She waited there rubbing her painful shoulder until the crunch of horses' hoofs on the gravel drive outside told her that her cousin was on his way.

*

"My dear, that is a very fetching blue," remarked Lady Hartwell, as they sat together in the parlour.

"How generous of my grandson to bring back such lovely gowns for you from York. But I hope, Elissa, that he has not been prevailing upon you to choose any more winners!"

"He did ask me. But I told him I could not do it," Elissa responded, for she could think of nothing better than the truth to tell her grandmother.

Then she started, as Lady Hartwell reached across and laid a hand on her arm, which was something she had never done before.

"I am so glad, my dear. He *must* not gamble as he does – and, although I am glad he has had such a big win, I know that it will make him want to go and win more and more!"

Elissa felt suddenly cold.

"I wish I had never had that dream!" she cried, the words slipping out before she could stop herself.

"What do you mean, girl?"

Elissa told her how she had fallen asleep and seen the dove's feather falling into her lap.

"So – I just – when I saw the horse's name – *Wings of a Dove* – I had a strange feeling and I just had to say the name, but I didn't think it could possibly win!"

Lady Hartwell's eyes grew deep and thoughtful.

"Do you have other dreams, like this?" she asked in a low voice.

Elissa nodded and told her, stumbling over all her words, about the other dream, where she had seen the date of her father's death.

Lady Hartwell looked interested.

"My daughter, Helena, your mother, had just such dreams. Sometimes I look at you and wonder where you have come from and if you really are part of our family. But now I know that you are. It pains me always to think of Helena – but at least, now that you have come, a little part of her too has returned to me."

"I do not see her in my dreams anymore, but it feels as if she is here with me," whispered Elissa.

Lady Hartwell's eyes glowed brightly now, but she did not shed the tears that were gathering.

Instead she gripped Elissa's hand.

"Be careful, my dear," she cautioned her, "I love Falcon dearly, but he is impetuous, and sometimes greedy. Do not let him force you to use this insight that comes to you for his own selfish purposes."

"I shall not, Grandmama, and I really don't think I could, even if I wanted to!"

She realised with horror she had just called Lady Hartwell 'Grandmama' – and waited to be reproved, but the old lady said nothing.

Elissa's fears subsided and a small flame of joy lit inside her.

What was it her Mama had said in the first dream she had just before her Papa died?

"*A time of great happiness is coming to you –* "

Somehow in spite of her cousin's anger and cruel behaviour towards her, she knew that she must remember those words and hold onto them, however difficult the way might be.

CHAPTER EIGHT

"We've made it to the top, Nelson!" cried Elissa, hugging the little dog in her arms.

She had been carrying him for almost half-an-hour, as his short legs had given up the struggle when the little path climbed steeply to the summit of the hill.

Now they were standing among tall craggy rocks, and the sunlit valley that lay below was revealed for the first time.

It was wonderful, at long last, to have arrived here at the end of the secret trail – and the only issue that now troubled Elissa was the blue cotton dress she was wearing for her walk.

When she had awoken with sunshine streaming in through her bedroom window and Ellen had brought in the dress – her cousin's gift – it had seemed quite perfect.

Now Elissa was alone and as she remembered her Papa, she wished that Ellen had not persuaded her to wear the dress, for no one, surely, would consider vivid sky blue to be a suitable colour for a girl in mourning.

But then she gazed at the deep valley below and she caught her breath with amazement, her sadness forgotten.

A forest of broken stone columns and crumbling walls rose up from the banks of a stream, where sunlight sparkled off the flowing water.

"How beautiful!" she sighed to Nelson. "But I am sure I have seen this view somewhere before – "

The pug wriggled out of her arms and set off down the hillside towards the ruins barking joyfully.

Elissa realised that she should not stay out for much longer as she must return to The Towers in time for tea, but she could not stop herself from following after him and her blue skirt flared out behind her as she ran down the path.

As she reached the bottom, her feet sinking into the soft lush grass, she thought again that the smooth stones of the ruined walls seemed strangely familiar.

It was very still and the only sound she could hear was the tinkling music of the stream as it coursed by.

"What a wonderful place! Oh, Nelson – wouldn't it be lovely to live here? It is so peaceful and the hills are all so beautiful, I could sit and look up at them all day."

She looked down, expecting the pug to be sitting at her feet, but he was not there.

"Nelson?" she called out, searching the long grass, but he had vanished without trace.

"Hey!" a man's voice shouted from the far side of the valley.

Elissa jumped with shock.

Was it her cousin riding back from the races?

She was about to scramble back up the steep path she had just descended, but she thought that, if she did so, she would be clearly visible to whoever had just called out.

And she could not leave without Nelson.

She called his name again as softly as she could and stepped behind one of the crumbling stone pillars to hide herself, hoping that the little dog would come and find her.

To her great relief, after a moment, she heard an excited bark.

Then a small object came flying through the air and Nelson's white body came racing after it.

"Nelson! Here!" hissed Elissa, but to no effect as the little dog was busy snuffling around in the grass.

Someone was whistling for him and Nelson trotted back towards the sound, carrying an object that looked like a pine cone in his teeth.

Sooner or later, whoever was playing with Nelson must surely come looking for her and Elissa decided that she would rather not wait, hiding like a scared child, but should step out from behind the pillar and reveal herself.

As she did so, her heart beating fast, she saw that there was a figure sitting underneath some fir trees in front of a wooden easel.

He wore baggy trousers and an old felt hat, just like her father used to do and for a moment she thought that it *was* him.

But, of course, it was not her Papa, it could not be him and neither was it a ghost for now he was standing up.

She saw, as he took off his felt hat to greet her, that he was a young man with brown hair and a wide smile on his tanned face.

"Forgive me, but I think your faithless little pug has decided that I am his best friend!" he called across to her. "I should never have thrown that pine cone for him."

As she came closer, his smile faded and turned to a look of complete astonishment.

"This I just don't believe!" he exclaimed. "It's you! Elissa Valentine. Don't you remember me?"

It was the young man who had come to the house in St. John's Wood on the day she had left for Yorkshire.

"Yes – of course!" she faltered, her voice unsteady from the shock of seeing him.

"I had no idea it was you," said Richard, "but I saw someone flying down the path and I thought a little piece of the sky had fallen! Your dress is exactly the same blue."

To her embarrassment, Elissa felt her eyes filling with tears.

The sight of him only a few moments ago looking so incredibly like her Papa had reminded her again of her bereavement and she felt guilty once more for not wearing her old black dress.

"What have I said? Don't you like your gown?" Richard now asked her, seemingly surprised.

Elissa fought back her tears and explained why she did not feel happy wearing the dress – even though it was the same brilliant hue as the glorious spring sky.

"But your father loved bright colours, so how could you lack respect for him by wearing blue?"

What he said was so true and so kindly spoken that a tear spilled over and ran swiftly down Elissa's cheek and she wiped it away, hoping he had not noticed.

If Richard had seen that she was crying, he made no mention of it. Instead he asked her where she was staying, and what had happened to her since they last met.

She explained all about Fellbrook Towers and Lady Hartwell.

"Are you happy there?" enquired Richard. "Is your grandmother kind to you? "

"She – is indeed very kind and I have every luxury I could wish for – "

Somehow, she did not want to say how cold Lady Hartwell had been to her and she certainly could not bring herself to speak about her cousin to this young man.

Richard was laughing.

"You have a much easier billet than I! Luncheon *al fresco* with bread-and-dripping is my lot and I am sure my landlady *means* to be kind, but persuading her to say even one word to me is impossible!"

Elissa noticed that the long rays of the sun were slanting through the ruined walls in a dramatic fashion.

"Do you come here to paint every day?" she asked.

He nodded.

"Papa would have loved this place," she sighed.

Richard was suddenly serious.

"I think of your father often. He is my inspiration. And sometimes, when I am sitting here, I almost feel him looking over my shoulder!"

Elissa gave a little shiver and she told him how, years ago, her Papa had lived in Yorkshire.

"So he might have come here too?"

Richard's eyes were shining.

"I'm sure I have seen sketches of a ruined building, just like this, among Papa's old drawings," said Elissa. "I thought I recognised the view as I came down the hill."

The two of them stood in silence marvelling at the coincidence that had brought Richard to the very same spot where Leo Valentine had painted so long before.

"I wish I could stay here instead of at my lodgings," Richard murmured after a while. "Wouldn't it be the most perfect place to live?"

"I had just the same thought only a few moments ago," Elissa answered, and, as she spoke, she was dazzled by the same golden light she had seen in her dream and the green hillside in front of her shimmered like a silken veil.

"What is it, Elissa? You have gone so pale!" asked Richard, sounding worried.

Elissa blinked.

For a moment she had just seen a beautiful building emerge from within the golden light with its pale walls and wide high windows.

"It's nothing," she told him. "Sometimes I think I see things or perhaps I dream them and I thought that I saw a house just here on the side of the hill."

"I expect that's because we were saying we would like to live here," smiled Richard.

"I suppose so."

Richard was looking at her so kindly that she found herself telling him about her recent dream of the dove's feather and how it had led to her winning a fortune for her cousin.

Richard's jaw dropped in amazement.

"That was *you*, was it! I heard the story of your cousin's win at my lodgings. Please, Elissa, if you do have any more dreams – tell me! I could use some ready cash myself!"

And he burst out laughing again.

She gazed at his handsome face, tanned from many hours spent in the open hair and he stopped laughing and looked back at her with his deep blue eyes.

He was so full of life and energy that standing next to him made her heart beat swiftly and her head feel light.

He could not possibly be more different from her dark-browed tempestuous cousin.

"I don't think that I can control my dreams," she replied. "They just come to me sometimes. And now – it must be tea time – I should think about returning."

"Elissa, may I accompany you? I think you might need someone to carry your little pug – he is wiped out!"

Nelson was lying in the shade of a fir tree, panting heavily.

"But your easel and all your paints!"

Elissa's face was growing hot and she did not know if she wanted him to come with her or not.

She would almost rather have walked back on her own, picturing his smile and recalling his vibrant voice, than have him still at her side, so warm and bold and eager, making her feel almost giddy with his presence.

He was determined to come with her.

"Oh, look – I shall just fold everything up and leave it here under this tree. Who is going to come and steal it out here?"

And then they were clambering up the steep track.

When they were over the hilltop and strolling down the green path on the other side, Richard enquired,

"Tell me more about this gentleman, your cousin."

A wave of confusion filled Elissa's head.

How could she possibly explain about Falcon and how afraid she was that he might put more pressure on her to choose another winning horse for him?

"Oh, you are blushing," exclaimed Richard, looking at her. "Perhaps there is something you have not yet told me about this cousin of yours?"

He was clearly teasing her, his eyes crinkling with amusement.

How could she tell him what had happened in the library that morning? She felt so ashamed and distressed as she remembered how Lord Hartwell had threatened her.

"I – " she began. "My cousin is – "

But her words tangled up in her throat and would not come out.

"Now you are going red! You are fond of him! Of course you are! Oh, foolish me!"

Richard struck himself on the side of the head in a mocking gesture of despair.

"And I thought I may have asked to see you again!"

"No, no, please – "

Now her words were flowing freely again,

"I should love to see you again. It has been such a pleasure to talk to you about Papa and – "

Richard's blue eyes became intensely bright as he looked at her.

"Then I am a very happy man!"

They walked on in silence for a while until the dark mass of The Towers came into view below them.

"So this is where you live, Elissa. It looks almost like a fortress or a prison with those great battlements on the top!"

"It is just a very fine house, but it is good to escape sometimes."

Richard turned towards her and took her hand as they walked up to the door in the garden wall.

"Do you think that you might just be able to escape tomorrow?" he asked, stepping back and letting go of her hand.

Elissa nodded, wishing that she could go on feeling the warmth of his fingers against her palm.

"I will meet you here then at two o'clock."

And he smiled as he passed over Nelson, who had been snuggled in the crook of his arm.

"Yes," Elissa murmured, "*tomorrow*!"

And he was gone, striding back up the path towards the hills.

As Elissa stepped through the door in the wall, she noticed a flash of movement from one of the windows on the first floor, as if a curtain had been pulled aside.

'Perhaps one of the parlour maids is dusting there,' she reckoned, as she made her way to the front door.

It was quiet and cool in the hall and she thought with relief that her cousin Falcon must still be at the races.

She stood still for a moment with her eyes closed picturing Richard, imprinting the memory of his handsome tanned face in her mind and remembering the warmth of his hand against hers.

"My dear girl!" the bell-like tones of Lady Hartwell interrupted her daydream. "I was hoping as it is such a lovely day that we might partake of tea on the terrace, but the hour is long past."

"Grandmama! I am very sorry! I forgot the time."

Lady Hartwell descended the staircase in a rustle of violet silk skirts.

"So easy to do when the sun is shining."

Her black eyes were very bright as she approached Elissa.

"Perhaps you will take a little turn about the garden with me before the sun falls too low in the sky?"

She reached out to take Elissa's arm.

After so long in the fresh air and so much exercise, Elissa would far rather have sat down to drink several cups of tea, but she could not refuse her grandmother's request.

"My dear," Lady Hartwell began, as they strolled among the neatly trimmed flowerbeds. "I saw you speaking to a young gentleman a few moments ago."

A cold finger of dark apprehension touched Elissa's heart, as she remembered the twitching curtain.

"Yes – he is someone who I knew in London – " she explained, striving to stay calm and keep her voice level. "Richard Stanfield."

"What a coincidence you should meet him again in Yorkshire!"

A curious little smile hovered over Lady Hartwell's lips and she spoke in a low gentle voice.

She did not appear angry and Elissa found herself relaxing. Perhaps at last her grandmother's coldness had thawed.

"And what is he doing here?"

"Oh – the scenery here is so wonderful – and he wants to be a painter."

Elissa felt her grandmother's hand tighten on her arm, as she continued,

"Richard is a gentleman and – he has fallen on hard times and thus he is trying to make a go of it as an artist."

Lady Hartwell fell silent, turning away from Elissa to look at the flowers.

After a few moments she spoke again.

"Ah – delightful! The first violets are opening, my favourite flower. But I think it is a little chilly now. Let's go inside, my dear."

And since she said nothing further about Richard, Elissa hoped that her curiosity was now satisfied and she had forgotten all about him.

*

Her cousin did not return to The Towers until some hours later and Elissa was alarmed when, shortly after she had heard the crunch of horses' hoofs on the gravel, there was a loud knock at her bedroom door.

Ellen ran to answer, but it was not Lord Hartwell standing outside, just a footman with an armful of brown paper parcels and several large hatboxes.

Ellen's eyes were wide as saucers as she took them from him.

"Shall I open them up, miss?" she asked excitedly.

"Please wait, Ellen," replied Elissa, as the footman bowed low in front of her and placed a white envelope in her hand.

But Ellen was already opening a hatbox to reveal a little grey velvet hat with long silvery plumes.

"His Lordship must 'ave 'ad good luck again," she sighed, stroking the hat.

That undoubtedly must be the explanation for this second delivery of gifts.

But her heart was beating with apprehension as she opened the envelope and read the note inside and there was no mention of another lucky win.

"*Sweet cousin,*" she read.

"*My bad behaviour this morning was inexcusable. I have been in hell all through today, completely unable to forget the expression of misery on your lovely face as I left the library.*

It is my dearest wish that you should accept these few small tokens as an expression of my sincere regret for causing you even a moment's distress.

I just cannot forgive myself for my intemperate and unkind words and I am sure I would not deserve that you should ever be able to do so.

But if you could find it in your heart to forgive – please, please dear cousin, wear the white-and-silver gown to dinner tonight and I shall know that I am in some small part forgiven for my cruelty and that you are truly an angel of mercy and kindness.

Your humble and penitent cousin,

Falcon."

A faint scent of whisky and cigars arose from the thick cream-coloured paper, as if the note had only just left Lord Hartwell's hands.

'Perhaps he really regrets treating me so roughly,' surmised Elissa.

Her shoulder was still painful from her fall that morning, but as she reread her cousin's words she recalled how sometimes his dark eyes with their swooping brows and the strong bones of his handsome face reminded her of her Mama.

Now Ellen was tearing yards of tissue paper from an exquisite white gown that was laced with silver brocade and embroidered with seed pearls.

"Did you ever see anything so lovely!" she gasped.

The dress was as soft and light as a cloud and Elissa could not resist reaching out to touch the delicate silk.

Maybe his bad temper and his thoughtlessness were just a small part of him, made worse by the fact that he had drunk too much champagne and whisky the night before.

'I should forgive Falcon,' she reflected. 'He is my cousin, part of my family and he has made an apology.'

She turned to Ellen.

"You are right, it is lovely. I shall wear it tonight!"

The dining room was filled with candles and the long table was dressed with white hyacinths and the same tiny violets Elissa had seen earlier in the garden.

As she sat down she felt a moment of unease as the white dress left her shoulders bare and she had not thought, as Ellen was dressing her, that her cousin would be seated opposite her.

Lord Hartwell's dark eyes were soft and unreadable in the candlelight without any hint of their usual boldness.

His only concern seemed to be that Elissa should enjoy her food, that her glass should always be filled and that everything should be just as she liked it.

Lady Hartwell sat silent at the table, a little smile on her lips and she ate very little.

As the dessert was brought in, she rose to her feet.

"I have no appetite for meringues," she sighed. "It has been a long day and I think, dearest, that I shall retire."

Lord Hartwell stood and bowed low over her hand.

"Rest well, dear heart."

Elissa stood up too as if to follow her grandmother.

"Oh no, Elissa," Lady Hartwell now insisted, a little smile flickering over her lips again, as she turned to leave. "You must stay and enjoy yourself."

Lord Hartwell gazed at Elissa as he crumbled his frosty white dessert with his fork.

"So I am clearly not forgiven," he remarked after a moment, the candle flames glinting in his dark eyes.

"Why – I – " Elissa began.

"For you cannot even bear to spend a few moments alone with me," he continued.

"Not at all – no – I just thought Grandmama – "

Elissa stumbled over the words in her confusion.

"But perhaps you are tired, your sweet face is very pale."

He stood up from the table and held out his hand.

"Come, let's go to the drawing room where we may be a little more comfortable."

"I should retire – " Elissa tried to say, but he was bearing down upon her, pressing her hand upon his arm and leading her out of the dining room.

Once in the drawing room he flung himself down into a leather armchair and propped his head in his hands, a smouldering frown creasing his brow.

"Why are you so cold to me!"

His voice was tight and hard.

Elissa's head was spinning.

"I – don't mean – " she began and suddenly he was kneeling on the carpet at her feet, catching her white silken skirts in his hands.

"It is all my fault!" he muttered. "I have been so heartless, thoughtless and cruel to you."

Then he looked up at her and more strongly than ever, she saw the likeness to her dear beautiful Mama in his handsome face.

He pressed his face against her skirts.

"Elissa, Elissa – " he mumbled and a tremor passed through his body that made her wonder if he was weeping.

"I forgive you," she then whispered, wishing that he would let her go.

He raised his head, his eyes glowing with a wild light.

"Marry me Elissa, my darling angel! *Promise that you will be my wife!*"

"Oh, but – I – "

Shocked to the core by his words and the strange brightness in his eyes, Elissa tried to move away from him, but he wrapped his arms around her knees and pulled her tightly towards him.

"Sweet angel – I can see by your gentle looks that you take pity on me!" he blustered, gazing up at her.

"But – "

"There shall be no 'buts'," he murmured, getting to his feet and catching hold of her bare shoulders. "So sweet an angel cannot help but love me."

And before she could utter another word, his lips were roughly pressed against hers and the heat of his body surged through her trembling limbs.

Elissa felt that she might suffocate if he did not take his mouth from hers, but just as suddenly as he had seized her, he let her go.

"My darling angel!" he said, a proud smile on his face. "You are white with exhaustion. Go to bed. And I – poor Falcon shall lie awake with thoughts of you – "

And as he sprawled across the armchair, his black eyes were fixed on her as Elissa stumbled to the door and escaped from the drawing room.

CHAPTER NINE

It had been the longest morning in Richard's life.

His mind kept leaping ahead to two o'clock and all he could see in his mind's eye was Elissa's lovely face, as she opened the door in the garden wall and stepped through it to join him.

He could not help feeling, as he set off to climb the hill path that he was undoubtedly the luckiest and happiest man in the world.

But when he did arrive expectantly at The Towers, Elissa was nowhere to be seen.

Richard pulled out his Papa's gold watch, which he had managed to keep when everything else from the house at Lanchberry Close was sold off and checked the time.

It was ten minutes to two.

'I am early!' he sighed with relief. 'She must still be at luncheon.'

As he waited patiently by the door in the garden wall, Richard smiled to himself, remembering how, when he heard Mr. Oldroyd's story, he had pictured the girl who chose the winning horse for Lord Hartwell to be a spoiled Society beauty.

This was not at all how Elissa had looked yesterday with her bright golden hair tumbling over the shoulders of her sky-blue dress, everything about her so fresh, innocent and entrancing.

He started as the front door of The Towers opened and a woman came out dressed in a smart silver gown and a grey hat.

She looked the epitome of an elegant Society lady as she stood on the long front step for a moment, shading her eyes with a grey-gloved hand, while the breeze ruffled the long silver feathers that dangled from her hat.

Now a tall gentleman with dark hair emerged and joined the woman on the front step, taking her arm.

He must surely be Elissa's cousin, Falcon, Richard thought. The man was tall and well built and, even from a distance, his strong features looked handsome.

But where was Elissa?

Surely she should be out in the garden by now and making her way to the door to greet him?

Now the couple by the door seemed to be arguing and the woman was trying to free her arm from the man's grasp.

Richard strained to hear what they were saying, but although he could catch the tone of their voices, the words were carried away on the warm spring breeze.

The man now seized the woman in his arms and, as he did so, her hat was knocked to the ground, revealing her golden hair, which was neatly tied up on top of her head.

For a moment Richard could not believe his eyes.

Then he tugged at the door in the wall until the iron bars at the top rattled, but it would not open.

"*Elissa!*" he shouted out.

It had to be her, despite the formal grey dress and the hat, clothes he could never have imagined her wearing.

No other girl had such brilliant golden hair.

She turned at the sound of his voice, and just for a moment, Richard thought she might break away and run to him, but the man caught her hand and pulled her back so that she was facing him again.

Richard remembered how Elissa had blushed when they had spoken about Lord Hartwell.

Yesterday he had made a joke of it.

But what if she did care for her cousin and had been too shy to tell him?

His heart now turned to ice as he watched the dark-haired man raise Elissa's hand to his lips.

He was drawing her close to him, pressing his lips to her face –

Richard could watch no more.

Elissa had not exactly lied to him, but she had not told him the truth. There *was* something between her and her cousin, Lord Hartwell.

Richard's mind was filled with a black and angry pain he could scarcely endure and he turned away from the garden and headed back towards the hills, stumbling over the heather and the rough grass in his eagerness to be gone.

*

"Please, please! Let me go!" cried Elissa, twisting her face away from the kisses her cousin was planting on her lips.

On the other side of the garden she had indeed seen someone looking through the door in the wall. It must be Richard, waiting for her – and with every inch of her body she longed to run to him.

"Why so distressed, my dear angel?" Lord Hartwell enquired, seizing her wrists.

She fought to free her hands, but he was too strong.

"I think perhaps we should go back inside, for your gown will tear if you keep behaving like this and since it is my gift to you, that would not be very polite, would it?" he snarled.

Elissa twisted her arms in a last desperate attempt to escape, but behind him the great door creaked open and Lady Hartwell appeared on the front step.

"What is going on?" she asked, her voice as sharp and cold as ice. "Cease this nonsense immediately, Elissa. Pick up your hat and come inside, I wish to speak to you."

Lord Hartwell let go of her and Elissa spun round looking for Richard.

He was no longer at the garden door and she could see him in the distance, running away up the path.

'Oh – I will never catch up with him,' she thought, her whole being sinking into despair.

"Did you not hear me?" Lady Hartwell shouted, her face pale with rage. "Come inside, girl! Now!"

Elissa picked up the velvet hat, from where it had fallen and followed her grandmother into the hall, her heart as heavy as a stone.

Lady Hartwell then led her to the rug in front of the great fireplace, where she had been waiting that very first night at The Towers.

"I have been far too lenient with you, Elissa," she said, spitting out the words.

"There has been a mistake, I did not mean – "

She thought perhaps Lady Hartwell was angry that Falcon had proposed to her or jealous that she had received so many fine gifts from him.

And yet it had been Lady Hartwell who had insisted that she wear the fine grey dress, the gloves and the hat this afternoon. Could it be that the sight of Elissa looking so elegant and refined had upset her?

Elissa began explaining that she had not accepted Falcon's proposal and had no intention of stealing Lady Hartwell's beloved grandson from her, and that she would not dream of marrying him.

But Lady Hartwell was not listening and carried on speaking in a cold angry voice,

"How could I have forgotten the bitter lesson your foolish Mama taught me? I should have never allowed you to leave this house!"

"But – I don't understand – "

"But history will not repeat itself. We have caught you in time!"

"I had no intention of running away!" cried Elissa, scared by the harsh expression on her grandmother's face.

"That is as may be!" she snorted, "but you will not be given the opportunity for any longer. Falcon will see to that. He has told me that he has proposed to you!"

A grim smile appeared on her lips.

"Yes – but I have not accepted," Elissa persisted, hoping her grandmother would now stop being so upset.

"Then I would advise you to do so immediately," Lady Hartwell replied, her mouth shutting like a trap as she finished speaking.

"I cannot!" gasped Elissa, shocked to the core, her limbs trembling uncontrollably.

Lady Hartwell appeared to be losing her mind.

Only yesterday she had gravely warned Elissa of her cousin's impetuous and greedy ways and told her not to allow him to take advantage of her.

Now, she was telling her to marry him!

Lady Hartwell was shaking her head, a look of grief and anger on her face.

"You expect me to believe you, when you say you did not mean to run away? I saw you with that young man yesterday. Hand in hand just like a pair of lovelorn fools. I know what will follow from such nonsense."

Oh, Richard!

Elissa's heart swelled with pain as she thought of him running away up her secret path.

What would she do if she never saw him again?

It was what her grandmother now wanted, that was abundantly clear.

She was afraid that Elissa would do exactly as her mother had done and turned her back on her family for the love of a poor artist.

And at that very moment she knew that she *did* love Richard with all her heart and soul, and she felt deep inside her that he loved her too.

Somehow, whatever it took, she must see him again and tell him how she felt.

Her grandmother was watching her closely.

"I can see it in your face that I am right," she was saying. "You are so innocent, so transparent. Unlike your devious wicked mother, who tricked me so easily."

Lady Hartwell sighed and smoothed her skirts.

"Well. There is an easy solution. You will marry Falcon. Perhaps that way I will keep some hold over him too. For he seems to adore you. I have never seen him so affected by a girl. Just think of all the gifts he has lavished on you!"

"I will give them all back!" cried Elissa, pulling off her grey kid gloves and throwing them to the floor along with the hat.

"*I cannot marry him.*"

"Go to your room at once," Lady Hartwell growled. "And stay there until you come to your senses. You will marry Falcon and you will remain here at The Towers, as is your duty."

"Well said, Grandmama!"

Lord Hartwell approached, from where he had been loitering by the door.

"My sweet angel, why are you weeping? All the girls in Yorkshire would give anything to marry me, didn't you know?"

He picked up Elissa's gloves and held them to his cheek, saying,

"Come, let me escort you to your room."

Desperate, Elissa looked at the great front door, but there were now two large footmen standing in front of it, and she knew if she tried to run, they would block her path.

She had no choice but to ascend the wide staircase with her cousin following close on her heels.

As they reached the landing he bent and muttered,

"The Towers is a grim old place for a sweet young beauty to be hidden away for ever. Take no notice of dear Grandmama. She means well, but I intend to take you to London. Pack your bags, my sweetest darling, as we will leave tomorrow. And you will need all the lovely clothes I have given you."

His breath felt hot on her face and Elissa recoiled from him.

She wanted to tell him that she could never marry him and she could not bear to go to London with him, but she was afraid that if she even looked at him, he might try to kiss her again.

They reached her bedroom door and Lord Hartwell fumbled in his pocket and drew out a silver key.

He was going to lock the door behind her.

A wave of panic surged through Elissa, but there was nothing she could do. If she confronted him, he would simply use force and she could not bear to feel his hands touching her again.

"*À demain*, my angel!" he sneered. "I shall leave you to reflect on your remarkable good fortune."

As she then stumbled blindly into her bedroom, she heard the key turn in the lock behind her, trapping her.

From the corridor outside, footsteps retreated and a faint sound of laughter echoed down the corridor.

*

Next morning, Richard awoke to the smell of bacon cooking in the kitchen below, an unheard-of occurrence at Mrs. Oldroyd's.

He groaned as he rolled over in his narrow bed.

How could he have slept?

Last night he had gone to bed in such an agony of body and soul that he was sure that he would remain wide awake until the cock in Mrs. Oldroyd's hencoop crowed.

But exhaustion must have overcome him and now the sun was up and shining brightly.

He groaned yet again as the picture of Elissa in the arms of her dark-haired cousin swam before his eyes again.

'I just cannot believe it, I cannot!' he whispered to himself as he had done so many times since those terrible moments yesterday afternoon.

The smell of bacon grew stronger and reluctantly he dressed and went downstairs.

"How do laddie," Mr. Oldroyd welcomed him from where he sat behind a large plate of bacon and eggs.

"Good morning. We do not usually see you here at breakfast, Mr. Oldroyd."

"Ah!" he grunted. "I must drive 'is Lordship and the young lady to London today. The Missus always cooks bacon if I'm to be away."

Mrs. Oldroyd had just put a plate of crispy rashers in front of Richard, but he could not touch them.

His whole body had turned cold with foreboding.

"Who? What young lady – ?" he stammered.

"His fiancée!"

He stared at Richard, surprised at his distress.

"Aye, laddie – they're to be married, Lord Hartwell and that poor young cousin of 'is."

"What do you mean?" Richard caught hold of Mr. Oldroyd's arm. "Why do you call her '*poor*'?"

Mr. Oldroyd put down his fork and turned to face Richard.

"He's a fine gentleman, Lord Hartwell, but he 'as a devilish temper if he don't get 'is way."

"But – surely she must love him if she – is to marry him – "

Richard hated the thought so much that the words stuck in his throat.

"I would not know, sir, for such matters are not my concern. But nowt at all will come of frettin' on an empty stomach – eat up, lad!"

"You are very kind, but I am not at all hungry," said Richard. "Mr. Oldroyd – I must go to The Towers – "

"Wait a little, sir, and eat your bacon, and then you can come with me in the dog cart."

But Richard was already on his feet and heading for the door while Mrs. Oldroyd watched him with her mouth hanging open in surprise.

"Do you have a horse or a pony I might borrow? I really cannot wait!"

"Take the little brown mare, Minnie, if you must," the coachman told him. "She's surefooted on the 'ill and that is the quickest way since you be in such 'urry."

Richard raced out into the bright spring morning.

He found Minnie tied up by the barn.

He leapt onto her without stopping to saddle up and headed at a gallop for the path that lead over the hill and to The Towers.

*

Richard pulled the iron doorbell expecting that they would turn him away, but as soon as he gave his name to a footman, the door opened and he was ushered inside.

"I am glad you have come," the tall old woman said in greeting and her silvery voice rang through the hall.

She smiled graciously at Richard.

"We must talk privately – will you come with me to my parlour?"

He followed her rustling purple skirts, breathing in a sweet scent of violets and was very aware that there was mud on his boots and his clothes smelled of horse sweat.

But Lady Hartwell's manner was exquisitely polite as she led him on into her private sanctum and ordered her maid to bring coffee.

"So, you are a friend of my granddaughter?" she began, her dark eyes fixed on his face.

"Yes – I knew her in London and I – am a friend of her family and a great admirer of her father."

He was about to ask her if he could speak to Elissa, when the maid appeared and offered him a gold-and-white china cup filled with steaming coffee.

"Oh!" he exclaimed, as he took the first sip, as it was just as he loved it, strong and fragrant. It was the best coffee he had tasted since he had been in South America.

"Do tell me about yourself – Mr. Stanfield," Lady Hartwell continued. "You are a painter, I believe?"

Richard explained that he was just starting out, but that he had already placed one of his works in a prestigious London gallery.

"But Lady Hartwell, I did not come to talk about myself. I – would like to see Elissa."

"That is not possible."

"But – "

"My granddaughter is not at home."

Richard felt his face grow warmer.

"I saw her here yesterday. And she cannot have left for London yet."

Lady Hartwell frowned.

"Who told you she is going to London?"

"Why, Mr. Oldroyd – the coachman."

"A gentleman should not listen to servants' gossip."

"I am sure that's right, Lady Hartwell, but I *must* see Elissa, I must speak to her before she leaves."

"She is *not* at home."

"She is still here – I know she is!" Richard jumped to his feet, but Lady Hartwell remained motionless, sitting on the sofa with her hands in her lap.

"When I say that she is not at home, Mr. Stanfield, I mean that she is not at home *to you*."

"But – I – "

"Do you love my granddaughter, Mr. Stanfield?"

Richard was not expecting this.

"Yes!" he replied immediately.

"Do you care about her future, her well-being and happiness?"

Lady Hartwell's voice was soft almost tender.

Richard sat down again.

"I do! That's why I am here. I love her and I – "

"You are a gentleman, Mr. Stanfield?"

"Yes!"

Richard caught sight of his boots, which had left a muddy mark on the parlour carpet.

"Well – I apologise for my appearance, but – "

"And you have a fortune?"

Richard's face now burnt with embarrassment.

"Not exactly – "

Lady Hartwell shook her head.

"You do not? Now young man, listen carefully, as I am going to tell you a pertinent story. Once upon a time, a beautiful young woman fell in love with a penniless artist, a bold and handsome man just like yourself."

Richard listened to her with growing horror as she told him how her daughter, the beautiful Helena Hartwell, had run away and how, unsuited to the harshness of life on a low income, she had sickened and died.

"And this is the life that you would ask my precious granddaughter to share with you, is it? No food, no decent place to live, no servants to wait on her?"

"But Elissa – wouldn't mind – " he stammered.

"And you call yourself a gentleman!" sneered Lady Hartwell.

"Do think, Mr. Stanfield! My grandson, her cousin, just adores her and will give her every luxury, everything she desires. How long do you think she would love you, when she must mop your floor and wash your dishes every day? How can you even think of asking her to live like that?"

Richard could not answer her.

He remembered Elissa in the garden yesterday, so very elegant in the fashionable grey dress, the gloves and the extravagant feathered hat.

It might be many years before he could buy her such lovely expensive luxuries, if indeed, he ever could.

But, far worse than that, what if he was unable to care for her, to keep her warm, to feed her, to give her the basic necessities of life?

The picture that Lady Hartwell had painted for him of the death of Lady Helena had struck deep into Richard's soul.

So, when the old woman rose gracefully from the sofa and asked if he was ready to leave, he nodded silently.

As he then set off on Minnie to ride back over the hill, he heard a crunch of hoofs and a rattle of wheels over gravel.

A closed coach, pulled by four black horses, was speeding down the drive that led away from The Towers.

'Elissa!' he whispered, as his heart leapt inside his chest. '*Goodbye, my darling.* Be happy!'

He could never give her a fine carriage and sturdy horses to pull it. He did not even own the rough little pony he was riding on now.

All he had in life was his art, his work and the tiny allowance that was just enough to keep him going.

But his love of art was little consolation as he rode back over the hillside and he felt deeply sad and lonely.

Even the beauty of the valley as he rode down into it on the other side of the hill could not raise his spirits.

'I can't stay here,' he thought. 'She will come back to The Towers when she is married and I could not bear to think of her so near. It's time to move on.'

He dug his heels into Minnie's sides and urged her forward, so that he could return to the cottage and pack his bags as soon as possible.

*

Mercedes de Rosario stepped out of the lift and into the lobby of the smart hotel in Mayfair, her red silk skirts sweeping over the marble floor.

The lobby was now thronged with fashionable and elegant people, but Mercedes ignored them, looking only for the handsome young man who had been following her around over the last few days and who seemed to turn up everywhere she went.

He was not there this morning and although there were several other gentlemen who looked as if they would like to talk to her, she could not help feeling disappointed as she sat down on one of the hotel's striped sofas.

"You look so sad, what's wrong?"

With a flounce of yellow skirts, Mercedes' younger sister, Dolores, came to join her.

"My boy is not here, you know him, the one who follows me everywhere," Mercedes pouted.

Dolores was as pretty as Mercedes with huge eyes and shining black hair.

Since they had arrived from Buenos Aires several weeks ago, the two Argentinian girls had attracted a great deal of attention.

"Oh, he is nobody, Mercedes!" Dolores rolled her eyes impatiently. "Just remember you are here to marry a Lord or maybe even a Duke."

She nudged Mercedes as an elderly gentleman with white hair and an eagle's beak approached the sofa.

"The Duke of Welminster!" Dolores hissed in her sister's ear. "His wife died last year."

The Duke bowed over Mercedes' hand and asked her if she would care to accompany him to the opera that evening.

But Mercedes was staring over his shoulder at the entrance to the lobby.

Her handsome young follower had just come in and was making his way to the bar.

"Please excuse me," she said to the Duke. "I have an appointment. Perhaps my sister would go with you?"

She rose rapidly from the sofa, leaving the Duke with Dolores and made her way to the bar.

"Who are you?" she asked, gazing into the young man's brown eyes.

"My name's Milward," he answered and, taking her hand, gave a little bow. "Montgomery Milward, everyone calls me 'Monty!'"

As she felt his hand touching hers, Mercedes' heart gave a little flutter. Now that at last she was standing close to him, he was even better looking than she had thought.

"I am Señorita Mercedes de Rosario," she told him.

"Yes, I know," he replied with a little smile.

CHAPTER TEN

The clamour of voices hushed to a low murmur as Elissa entered the ballroom at the Piccadilly Hotel where Lord Hartwell was hosting a party to celebrate his return to London and his engagement to her.

She could hear the whispers of the people standing close by,

"Why, it's *her*! His new fiancée! They say she has won him a fortune at the races!"

Elissa's heart shrank with misery.

She knew that she had never looked as impressive as she did tonight, her ice blue gown was sparkling with diamonds and her golden hair was dressed in a magnificent cascade of curls.

But there was no kindness in Lord Hartwell's eyes as he approached and took her hand in a cruelly tight clasp.

She remembered how all afternoon he had paced up and down in the elegant suite of rooms he had rented for her overlooking the busy thoroughfare of Piccadilly.

"Why will you not do it?" he had hissed, thrusting a crumpled copy of *The Racing Times* into her hand. "What more do you want from me? I have given you everything – including myself! *Just pick me another winner*!"

Cold chills had run all through Elissa's body as she tried to explain that she had no control over her ability to predict events. It was just something that would come to her when she was least expecting it.

"You are lying!" he exclaimed. "I have spoken to Grandmama – she tells me you have the power to foretell the future. It's a gift that runs in our family. God knows, I wish I had inherited it myself."

His face was dark red with rage as he gripped the arm of the sofa where she sat.

"Please, do not ask me to choose another horse for you," Elissa begged him, fighting to keep her voice from shaking. "You will lose the wager."

Lord Hartwell muttered a curse and struck the arm of the sofa with his fist.

Elissa shrank back from him, fearing that he might hit her, but he took a deep breath and swallowed his anger.

"My angel," he coaxed, "I know what it is. You are afraid that if we have another great success at the races, I will take the money and then not marry you after all."

"*No* – " Elissa tried to say, but her voice completely deserted her.

Lord Hartwell knelt in front of her, his fierce black eyes fixed on her face.

"You must not be afraid, sweet one. Tonight all of Society will be at the party I am giving for you. In front of all of them I shall renew my promise to make you my wife. Your reputation is totally spotless and your brilliant future is guaranteed."

And now the party was in full swing as she paraded in front of the assembled Society guests, her hand on Lord Hartwell's arm.

"Let them see you smile, cousin," he urged. "That is what they will expect, for they know you are wearing the most expensive gown in London."

Elissa forced her trembling lips to comply with his request as she walked beside him, seeing little of the eager faces that loomed up to congratulate her.

Even the two young women, as vivid and gorgeous as tropical flowers in their bright silks, who duly curtseyed before her, lisping out their good wishes with a charming Spanish accent, escaped her notice.

"Now *that* is what I call a man!" Dolores confided in her sister, as Lord Hartwell moved away, continuing his circuit of the ballroom. "So very handsome. *And* – he is a Lord!"

"He is already spoken for, the girl on his arm is his fiancée," Mercedes told her and she turned away to search in the crowd for Monty, who had promised her he would be at this party tonight.

"Hmm." Dolores bit her full lower lip. "That cold little ice maiden will not be able to keep him for long!"

Her eyes flashed with excitement at the challenge she saw ahead of her.

Mercedes did not hear her, as Monty had just come in, handsome and dapper in his white tie and tails.

She hurried to him, dodging between the Lords and Ladies who blocked her way.

"Oh, Monty!" she sighed, as he raised her hand to his lips.

He was perfectly English, so cool, formal and polite and yet his brown eyes gazed at her in such a delicious way and the thrill that she felt as he kissed her gloved fingers glowed through her whole body.

"Señorita!" he breathed.

He turned away from her to introduce a young man who was standing behind him.

"I would like you to meet a good friend of mine. *Richard Stanfield.* I believe that you may have made his acquaintance already."

*

The bodice of her gown felt tight around Elissa's chest and her embroidered skirts dragged heavily as she followed Lord Hartwell around the ballroom.

'I cannot breathe and I shall suffocate if I do not get away,' she fumed.

Surely she must have nodded and smiled graciously to everyone at the party by now.

"I feel unwell – " she whispered to her cousin. "I should like some air – "

He shrugged.

"Go and stand by the door then and make sure you are nice to anyone arriving. They will not be impressed to see you looking miserable."

And he brushed her hand away from his arm.

As Elissa moved away from him, a girl in a bright magenta gown approached Lord Hartwell, her head on one side as her shining black curls hung enticingly across her bare shoulder.

'Maybe he will leave me alone for a few moments,' Elissa mused, relieved that someone else had attracted his attention.

In the very next instant the crowded throng of faces vanished and Elissa totally forgot the tightness of her dress.

For standing by the entrance to the ballroom was an elegant young gentleman in formal clothes, his blue eyes wide as he gazed at her in astonishment.

"Richard!" cried Elissa and gathered up her skirts to run to him.

But someone else was already distracting Richard's attention

It was a tall woman in a bright red dress that echoed the highlights in her glowing russet hair.

And now, to Elissa's horror, Richard was no longer looking at her, but was speaking urgently and passionately to this red-haired woman.

"I thought I would never see you again," she heard him say.

And the red-haired woman threw her arms around his neck and was weeping on his shoulder.

Elissa gave a little cry of pain.

It was as if her heart had broken apart inside her.

She did not linger to hear more, but ran from the ballroom, through the crowded lobby of the hotel, and out onto Piccadilly, where a soft spring rain was falling on the gleaming pavements.

"How do!"

A stout figure approached her.

"Oldroyd! What are you doing here?"

"Waitin' for 'is Lordship. He often likes to take a drive down to the East End late at night and make a wager on a cock-fight – or a rat-baitin'."

Elissa shivered with revulsion.

"How horrible!"

"Tis not a pleasant occupation, but many gentlemen enjoy such things. You should have your cloak, miss, in this mizzle."

Elissa felt cold drops of moisture falling onto her face and shoulders and she knew that the expensive gown would be spoiled.

But she would rather have died than gone back into the hotel where Richard was in the arms of another woman.

Oldroyd's brow was furrowed with concern.

"Shall I drive you somewhere, miss?" he asked.

She could see the dark shape of the coach-and-four by the pavement, the patient horses' heads hanging low as they waited.

Elissa swayed on the pavement and suddenly her head was full of a bright golden haze.

In the centre of the haze was a pretty little house, its white walls gleaming like snow and a beam of warm light shining out from the open front door.

"Take me home!" she exclaimed.

"Miss, it be three days' journey to Yorkshire!"

"No, no. Take me to St. John's Wood!"

Elissa clapped both her hands over her eyes trying to hold on to the heavenly vision of the little white house that had flashed so vividly into her mind, but it was already beginning to fade.

"Miss?"

Oldroyd laid a steadying hand on her arm.

"Please! I must go there, now!"

"Come, then."

The coachman wrapped his heavy overcoat around Elissa's shoulders and helped her into the coach.

"Hurry, please hurry!" she whispered, as the horses lurched forward, carrying her back to her old home.

*

"We need to discuss all this calmly and rationally," Monty now proposed, closing the door of one of the small private salons that led off the ballroom.

Mercedes' face was drenched with torrents of tears and hysterical sobs wracked her body.

Richard's stomach crawled with embarrassment.

"Monty, old man, can we just forget it?" he said. "I really don't care about the money anymore."

It was true, for all he could think of was the vision of Elissa, so cold and pale and astonishingly beautiful in the diamond-studded gown – Elissa, turning her back on him and hurrying out of the ballroom as if he did not exist.

Monty ignored Richard.

He sat down on one of the small gold chairs and pulled some papers out of his pocket.

"It is all perfectly simple, Señorita de Rosario," he began. "All you need to do is to transfer both the capital which you have misappropriated from Mr. Stanfield, plus the money which you have made from it while it has been in your possession and we will say no more about it."

"Oooh! I am ruined!" wept Mercedes.

"Perhaps now you will have some sympathy for the suffering that you caused to my friend, when you stole his fortune," Monty asserted, frowning at her.

"No, you – don't understand!" a fresh flood of tears were welling up in the Argentinian's eyes. "I will give the money back, but Monty don't look at me in that cruel way, I cannot bear it. I am *nothing* unless you can care for me."

"As I said, simply sign this paper, just here on the dotted line and we will say no more about it."

"I cannot bear it if you hate me!" she wailed and then turned to Richard.

"I am not a bad person! Please, tell your friend I would have given the money back to you! My family were so poor, I just needed to borrow it, to invest – and now I have three times as much! I will give it all to you!"

Richard looked appealingly at Monty, but his friend was not giving way and he was still holding the papers in front of Mercedes.

"Look here – old man. Cannot we let bygones be bygones?" suggested Richard. "If Mercedes will just give me back my Papa's legacy, I should be quite happy."

"Take all of it!" Mercedes wept. "Only, Monty, do not cast me out!"

"Is that what you want, Richard?" Monty asked him ignoring Mercedes. "Just the original sum of money with no interest?"

Richard nodded and Monty, with a distinct sigh of exasperation, picked up a pen and made some adjustments to the paperwork.

Mercedes had only just scrawled her signature at the bottom, when the salon burst door open and Lord Hartwell stormed in.

"Where is my fiancée?" he snarled, seizing Richard by his shirt. "What have you done with her, scoundrel?"

Mercedes gave out a cry of terror and threw herself onto Monty's lap, twining her arms around his neck.

"I have no – idea," choked Richard, because Lord Hartwell now had hold of his tie.

"She is certainly not here," came in Monty, "search the place if you don't believe me."

Lord Hartwell looked around at the tiny salon.

There was quite clearly nowhere to hide a woman in a ball gown.

"Very well," he grunted, giving a final sharp tug to Richard's tie before letting him go. "But your life will not be worth living if I find that you are in any way responsible for her disappearance."

The girl in a bright magenta gown appeared in the doorway of the salon, a bottle of champagne in her hand.

"Come back to the party now, your Lordship," she purred. "Your poor little fiancée, I think she must have the headache and has gone to lie down."

With a wink at Mercedes she slid her arm through Lord Hartwell's and drew him back into the ballroom.

"Miss, I cannot leave you here," moaned Oldroyd.

Elissa stood in the soft rain looking up at the house.

The walls had been repainted a pristine white, just as she had seen them in her vision and the garden path was lined with a row of pretty bay trees in tubs.

Someone had very clearly lavished a great deal of loving care and money on her old home.

But the front door stood firmly closed, not at all as she had seen it in her mind's eye.

"Please go, Oldroyd! Don't wait for me."

In spite of the closed door, something deep inside Elissa knew that she must stay here.

"Very well, miss. But you should keep my coat – and, miss, if 'is Lordship be on the warpath, I shall tell 'im the 'orses were fidgetin' and I took 'em for a trot round the block."

"Thank you so much, Oldroyd!"

She then reached out to clasp the coachman's rough hand and then he was gone.

Elissa pulled up the collar of Oldroyd's coat and waited in the rain as the rumble of the coach wheels faded.

Just as silence had returned to the street, the front door of the house opened.

Exactly as she had seen in her vision, a long ray of golden light spilled out down the garden path and then a tall thin man in a smoking jacket stepped out.

"Hello there!" he called. "I heard a coach come by and I wondered if we had a visitor!"

It was Mr. Harker, the art dealer.

Elissa pushed back the collar from her face and the light from the open door lit up her golden hair.

Mr. Harker gasped and held out his hand to her.

"Miss Valentine! At last. I have been searching for you everywhere!"

The hall seemed so different, as Elissa now stepped inside. It was very warm, as if fires were burning in all the rooms and from the walls, new gaslights shone with a soft bright light over a Chinese vase on a polished pedestal.

"Oh, dear Miss Valentine!" Mr. Harker exclaimed, as he lifted Oldroyd's heavy coat from Elissa's shoulders and saw the silk and diamonds that gleamed beneath.

"I have been so concerned for your welfare, when I could not trace you, but look at you! Obviously I need not have worried!"

"Mr. Harker! Dear Mr. Harker! Please – am I safe with you here? Can I trust you? I cannot go back – "

He then directed Elissa into the drawing room, now decorated in the Chinese style with painted wallpaper and led her to the sofa, where Mrs. Harker was sitting in front of a blazing fire.

Trembling with shock, Elissa explained what had happened since she had left London, and that tonight she had run away from her demented cousin, who was forcing her to marry him.

"My dear," Mr. Harker interrupted. "You must put all of this from your mind immediately. You are now in such a position that you will never need to be beholden to your family ever again."

"What do you mean?" Elissa asked, unable to make sense of his words.

"Elissa, your father's paintings are now selling for the highest prices in London. His work at long last has been discovered. You will never want for anything again."

"Enough!" Mrs. Harker, a plump woman in a rose-coloured gown, cried. "The poor girl is about to keel over

146

with the shock of it all. Come, dear, let me take you to our spare bedroom and tomorrow Gabriel will take you to the gallery and explain everything."

It was a long while before sleep came to Elissa that night.

She lay in her old bedroom, now the spare room, and though the swansdown pillows on the brand new bed were incredibly soft, they gave her no comfort.

Richard did not love her and the extraordinary good news that Mr. Harker had just given her meant absolutely nothing, for she felt as if she had nothing left to live for.

*

Elissa, wearing one of Mrs. Harker's best flowered gowns with a belt at the waist, as it was more than a little too big for her, and carrying a smart parasol, emerged from the office near the back of the gallery where she had been sitting with Mr. Harker for the last couple of hours.

He had taken her through the full inventory of her father's works, explaining when each had been sold and for how much and she now understood that she was a very rich woman indeed.

"Now I have to find another artist of your father's calibre! The walls are quite bare, as we have sold so many paintings in the last few weeks," declared Mr. Harker.

"Do you have anything of Papa's left?" she asked.

"One picture, which I cannot let go. A portrait of yourself beneath a cherry tree. Mrs. Harker and I love it, and I should like to take it back to the house one day and hang it there."

He pointed to a small side room, which led off the gallery and, her heart full of emotion, Elissa went to look at the picture.

A broad-shouldered young man had beaten her to it, and stood still in front of the picture, blocking her view.

Elissa gave a cry of shock and dropped her parasol, which fell to the floor with a clatter.

The young man then spun round and saw her and a multitude of emotions passed over his face – surprise and joy and doubt and then joy again.

"*Elissa*, Elissa, Elissa!" he called out fervently.

She wanted to run away, but her legs were too weak to carry her.

"Are you all right?" Richard was asking, "everyone is looking for you."

"I am – fine," she replied, holding her voice steady with a great effort.

A cloud passed over Richard's face.

"Your fiancé is incandescent with rage – "

"I have *no* fiancé."

Elissa bent to pick up the parasol.

She had to leave at once because she could not look at him any longer without breaking down and weeping.

Mr. Harker, who had been hovering just outside the room, now came in and stood protectively by Elissa.

"Good morning!" Richard greeted him, holding out his hand politely to the art dealer. "Richard Stanfield, you may remember me. I believe that you may have one of my paintings – Old Newman."

Recognition dawned on Mr. Harker's lean face.

"Mr. Stanfield! Of course. Forgive me. Alas, Old Newman is no longer with me. But you will be pleased to hear that it made an excellent price. I should like some more of your works, if you have any. Leo Valentine has had such a remarkable success these recent weeks and my walls are empty!"

"Can this be true?" Richard turned back to Elissa, his eyes wide with delight.

"Oh, yes." Mr. Harker explained. "Miss Valentine is now a wealthy woman, I am delighted to say."

"That is wonderful!" replied Richard and much to Elissa's surprise, he burst out laughing.

"But – what a strange coincidence! I do have some other paintings but my present circumstances have changed dramatically – and I, too, find myself quite well off. I am not so desperate for you to sell my work as I was last time I saw you, Mr. Harker!"

"But then you must not neglect your talent!" Elissa added, forgetting herself and catching hold of his arm.

"You love to paint – it's your life! Remember when I found you at the Old Priory, Richard!"

Richard took her hand in his, suddenly serious.

"I have thought of nothing else but *you* since you disappeared from my life."

Mr. Harker gave a polite cough and withdrew into the main gallery, leaving them alone.

Richard was speaking in a low voice, first telling Elissa just how much he had missed her and then going on to explain how Monty had found Mercedes and recovered his inheritance.

"But I should rather not have recovered my fortune, than lost you.

"And yet when I went to Fellbrook Towers to find you and your grandmother told me how hard life would be for you if you married me, a poor artist, I thought perhaps it was best that you married your cousin."

Elissa could not speak.

She could only shake her head.

Then, while she gazed into his eyes he saw the truth of her feelings for him, caught her in his arms and held her so close that time stood still.

"Monty, old man, are you free on the 18th of June?" Richard asked his friend, as they strolled together along the Embankment.

"Possibly," replied Monty. "Why do you ask?"

"Oh, you are becoming such a cagey old lawyer! Just say yes!"

"Not without knowing what I am agreeing to."

"I want you to be my Best Man!"

Richard slapped his friend hard on the shoulder.

Monty stopped in his tracks.

"You've really gone and done it! Congratulations, old man! Well, I was planning a little trip abroad for June, but I shall have to postpone it."

"Abroad, Monty? Where?"

"Argentina," he replied and a faint blush crept over his face.

Now it was Richard who stopped dead in his tracks.

"What?" he gasped.

"Señorita de Rosario has asked me to help her out with some business affairs," Monty told him looking rather embarrassed.

"Oh, Monty! *Please* be careful!"

"Don't worry, Richard, I shall. Mercedes won't be able to get anything over on me and she *is* rather glorious!"

Richard shook his head in despair.

A broad smile crept over Monty's face.

"I don't think you are in any position to advise me, Richard!" he laughed. "And yes, I will be delighted to be your Best Man."

*

"Everyone, but everyone has deserted me," Lady Hartwell stared up at Elissa from where she lay on the sofa in her parlour, "except for this creature!"

And she stroked the large ginger cat on her lap.

"Marmalade!" Elissa sighed, as the cat purred very loudly at her.

She remembered how he had come to her when she first arrived at The Towers, and suddenly felt very sorry for her grandmother. For if it was true that cats always went to those who most needed comfort, then Lady Hartwell must be feeling really bad.

"Falcon has run away to South America," the old woman was saying, her voice deep with grief. "They say the girl is very pretty and has money, but he has not even brought her to see me. Why, oh, why did *you* not marry him, Elissa?"

Nelson, hiding under Elissa's chair, reached up and licked her hand affectionately and his friendly gesture gave her the courage to speak the words that she had come to Yorkshire to deliver.

"I could not, because I am in love with Richard."

Lady Hartwell gave a small cry of exasperation, but Elissa continued with what she had to say.

"I did not know that such a Heaven of love and of happiness existed in the world – and now we have found each other, nothing will come between us, but Grandmama – please don't turn your back on us."

Lady Hartwell remained silent, scowling down at Marmalade.

"We are intending to live here in Yorkshire – just on the other side of the hill. Richard is going to build a beautiful new house for us – we will be your neighbours."

Lady Hartwell muttered something impenetrable about irresponsible impoverished artists.

"We are not poor, Grandmama, and we will come and see you every day – and Nelson and Marmalade too."

Elissa explained about the fortune that had come to her from her father's paintings and about Richard's family inheritance.

"There is only one thing we lack and that is your blessing."

"Oh, why should you care? Please yourself. What do I matter to you?" Lady Hartwell snapped.

For a moment Elissa wanted to stand up and leave, but she could not without one more attempt.

"Grandmama, I have lost almost all my family," she pleaded. "I could not bear to lose you too."

Marmalade's purr rose to a crescendo and suddenly he jumped down from Lady Hartwell's lap and strolled out of the parlour, his tail held as high as a banner.

Elissa could see a silvery track of a tear appear on her grandmother's cheek and her heart swelled with joy as the old woman reached out to take her hand.

*

The little Chapel at Fellbrook Towers had never looked so lovely as it did on the 18th of June. It was decked with pink and white roses that filled the air with a glorious fragrance.

Elissa looked around at the smiling faces of all those who had come to celebrate her marriage to Richard.

Not least among them her grandmother, proud and resplendent in a pale violet gown and magnificent feathered hat.

Monty, having carried out his duties as Best Man, was now at Lady Hartwell's side, no doubt promising her that he would look out for her grandson on his forthcoming trip to Argentina.

Mr. and Mrs. Harker were there and Elissa knew that they had brought with them, safely wrapped up in card and brown paper, her father's cherry tree painting, to grace the walls of her new home.

And in the back row of the pews, which had been assigned to the staff, Elissa caught a glimpse of Ellen.

Her eyes were shining with excitement from under the brim of her lace cap, and there too was Kitty, looking so proud at having travelled all the way from London to take up the position of housekeeper at their new home.

Elissa's heart was filled with golden light as she saw so much joy all around her and she remembered how her Mama had come to her in a dream and told her that a great happiness would be hers.

She closed her eyes, knowing that surely Mama must be with her now at this, the most wonderful moment of her life.

Then she turned to her new husband, feeling the heavenly warmth of his hand in hers as they walked back down the aisle together.

"You have brought me such happiness," she sighed.

"My darling Elissa – it is you who bring happiness wherever you go," murmured Richard.

Elissa thought of the long green path that stretched away over the hill leading to the site of their new house, where the foundations were already laid.

By the time they had returned from honeymoon, their beautiful home would be almost complete.

She suddenly realised that the path must always have been their very special trail to love, and that she only had to follow it wherever it led to find the wonderful happiness her mother promised her.

They stepped out of the Chapel into the bright June sunshine into a shower of confetti.

Elissa's heart and mind were filled with a vision of the joy and love that would be hers and Richard's.

It would radiate out from them to light up the lives of all who knew them.

As he reached to take her in his arms and kiss her, she was enveloped in a Heavenly bliss so great it was beyond all her imaginings.

"This is ours, for now and all Eternity!" she cried, as at last he released her.

"Forever and ever, my Love!" he answered and led her forward into their new life together.